Secret Me

Secret Me

ANGEL JENDRICK

JAMES LORIMER & COMPANY LTD., PUBLISHERS
TORONTO

James Lorimer & Company Ltd., Publishers acknowledges funding support from the Ontario Arts Council (OAC), an agency of the Government of Ontario. We acknowledge the support of the Canada Council for the Arts, which last year invested $153 million to bring the arts to Canadians throughout the country. This project has been made possible in part by the Government of Canada and with the support of Ontario Creates.

Cover design: Tyler Cleroux
Cover illustration: Jordan Masciarelli

Library and Archives Canada Cataloguing in Publication

Title: Secret me / Angel Jendrick.
Names: Jendrick, Angel, author.
Identifiers: Canadiana 20220485011 | ISBN 9781459417250 (hardcover) |
    ISBN 9781459417182 (softcover) | 9781459417410 (epub)
Subjects: LCGFT: Novels.
Classification: LCC PS8619.E52 S43 2023 | DDC C813/.6—dc23

Published by:
James Lorimer &
Company Ltd., Publishers
117 Peter Street, Suite 304
Toronto, ON, Canada
M5V 0M3
www.lorimer.ca

Distributed in Canada by:
Formac Lorimer Books
5502 Atlantic Street
Halifax, NS, Canada
B3H 1G4
www.formaclorimerbooks.ca

Distributed in the US by:
Lerner Publisher Services
241 1st Ave. N.
Minneapolis, MN, USA
55401
www.lernerbooks.com

Printed and bound in Canada.
Manufactured by Friesens Corporation in Altona, Manitoba, Canada in February 2023.
Job #294591

For Paige and Ava

01 Risks We Take

I LOVE THE RISK of getting caught.

Heart thumping, palms sweating, stomach-clenching kind of risk.

Catch me. Arrest me. *Do it.* I don't care.

I can barely make out the PA system over my pulse pounding in my ears with abandon, but I know the store is closing. I glance casually around me before adding the lipstick to the other stolen items in my purse.

Mine.

I leave the Charlottetown Walmart with a heavier load than when I went in, still feeling like something's missing as I pull on my toque and mitts. I need to think smarter when I shoplift, think *bigger*, because the stakes still aren't high enough. Not for my mother, the cop, to notice me. If I end up in the back of her police cruiser, maybe she'll remember the daughter she chose her job over. Sometimes I feel like I could literally disappear and it'd be days before she noticed.

Kind of a sad little reality, right?

I make my way to the sweet-sixteen birthday gift my dad bought me last year, when things were different — maybe better. Before he got a job out west and divorced Mom. With the mess of their split on my mind, I give the Camry's front tire a hard kick. Pain shoots up my leg and I wince, immediately regretting how stupidly impulsive I can be. Grumbling, and in a foul mood, I open the driver's door to trade my purse for the snow brush. As I'm limping around cleaning the snow off the car, I think of how good the South would be right about now. Gone are the days where I look forward to skating, hot chocolate, and sledding. Now, as soon as a hint of chill creeps into the air, I'm wishing I was one of those lucky snowbirds. A house in Florida would be epic.

By the time I'm finally slipping behind the wheel, my hands are nearly frozen off. I start the ignition — don't ask me why I didn't think to do it earlier — and crank the heat. I spend the next few minutes checking my phone, killing time while the windshield defrosts. I stare at the notifications, my shoulders slumping. During the half hour I was in the store I got ten messages and one missed video call, none of them from my mother. Go figure.

Sighing, I reach over and set my phone in the dash holder, dialling my best friend Aiden as I steer the car out of the nearly empty lot. I live close to Victoria Park, in the Brighton area. My house isn't the biggest on the block, but I like it. Besides my friends, it's been the only constant thing in my life the last couple years. I know I can go home and be myself, without fear of someone watching me, expecting something from me I'd rather not give. Don't get me wrong, most of the time I love my friends and the advantages that come with being at the top, but it can be taxing. The popularity you once craved begins stealing your uniqueness, your flair, everything that makes you you, until you're exactly like all the other pretty girls. You start to think like them, act like them, dress like them. Or at least that's the version you give to the rest of the world. The other, less acceptable versions are buried under sarcasm and flat-out bullying.

At home, at least I get to kick back in my too-large sweats and t-shirt and just be Tage. Every now and again, it takes me a bit to remember who she is. Funny how that happens.

Aiden answers on the second ring, her face and ginger hair filling up my screen. "'Bout time you rang me back," she greets me, letting out a giggle. I hear her boyfriend beside her, more people in the background. "Hayley's parents are gone for the night, and I'm pretty sure she snapped the entire senior class her party invite. That means you, biotch. Get over here and shake that ass!"

My excitement to get home bursts, and I try to hide my disappointment. Some nights I just want a quiet night in. Entertaining mean-drunk Hayley is a total buzzkill, but I already know it's exactly what I'll do. As tiring as the parties and games get, change, and the potential rock bottom that comes with it, doesn't appeal to me in the slightest. At least I know what to expect from Hayley and the gang.

"And, Tage? You still have your fake ID? We're running out of vodka."

* * *

Somehow, all of Hayley's parties end with me hating a little more of myself than I did hours before.

Not because of the cheer routines I'm pressured into showing off, or the fact that I constantly overdrink and never learn. No, the problem digs so much deeper than that, and it's only when I'm drunk that I let myself feel all the bullshit. I hate how weak-willed I am, how it's never gotten easier to bury or embrace my authentic self. I despise the fact I have no one I trust enough to open up to, not even my selfish parents. I've been friends with Hayley for years, and she openly hates the gays yet hasn't a clue a queer like myself hides in her circle. I don't have the balls to come out, not after what happened the last time I tried.

I think I hate that most of all. Tough, bitchy Tage cares more about acceptance than her own happiness.

"Girl, where you off to? Let's do another one!" Hayley grabs my hand, tugging me back into the circle the partiers have made around the three of us. My gaze finds hers, and the contents of my stomach give a slight churn at the thought of tumbling a third time. Somersaults, Smirnoff, and small spaces? Not a good mix.

"I don't … I feel a little sick," I admit. I had kicked off my heels some time ago and now have to squint to fully make her out. Everything is fuzzy, extra shiny, and her hair seems more angelic than I remember. She's so pretty it's disgusting, but that's where her beauty ends.

"Tage, you don't look so good," Aiden's boyfriend Dylan says as I push past our friends to head for the bathroom.

"Speak for yourself, Dylan," I reply, and my stomach does another flip. I'm betting puking is definitely in my future, but when I finally reach the second level, I catch a cool breeze from one of the bedrooms. Curious, I head toward it, immediately grateful the chill seems to be helping with my nausea. It's Hayley's brother's room, but he's working tonight so my guess is someone came up here to smoke. Taking a cautious seat on the bed, I close my eyes and inhale the crisp air.

Unfortunately, I'm not alone for long.

My gut has only just settled when my on-again-off-again boyfriend finds me hiding out. Ben stands in the doorway for a moment, letting his eyes adjust to the dim light before they land on me.

I sigh, not in the mood. I'm so tired of putting on a show for everyone. If I could just be myself, Ben wouldn't be the one coming to kiss me. I'd probably be playing video games somewhere or watching manga or whatever else emo nerds do. I'd be kissing someone, all right, but not Ben.

"Hey."

Ben stumbles in, smelling like beer and sporting a sloppy grin, and I watch as he falls onto the bed beside me.

"Hey, bae. What're you doing up here? Waiting for me?" His grin widens. With his straight, white teeth and playful blue eyes, every girl in my school is under the illusion I've hit the jackpot. 'Ben is so cute, so funny, so this, so that.'

He's not my type.

But they *don't* know the real Tage. Only one person in my entire school sees what and who I truly am. Wren, a nonbinary emo queer with a penchant for piercings and a smile to die for.

And I treat them like crap.

02 Friends and Allies

"SUNDAY CHEER, SUN-DAY cheer, y'all ready for some of that uh-uh cheer?!" Hayley shouts, letting out a whoop loud enough to have even the custodial staff glance over. A few feet away, Aiden and I are watching Hayley's LOL moment, and when she bends at the knees to start twerking in front of the All-Star Cheerleading class, Aiden erupts in a fit of giggles. I guess it's a good thing we wear spandex and not skirts, because Hayley's butt would be jiggling right out of her clothing.

"Hey, can we all focus here?" our coach, Leanne, calls out before raising a whistle to her lips. *Tweet, tweet!* "Hayley! Since you're so energetic, why don't you show everyone the mark through? Start from the top."

"Sure, Coach." Hayley nods, moving to get into position and not looking the least bit embarrassed she was called out. Hayley's always been an attention-seeker. She can be the life of the party if the mood suits her, but sometimes she can be downright cruel. Like, meaner than me, and trust that I've heard the gossip about how hateful I can be. I know some days I treat certain ... individuals harshly. Harsher than they deserve. Even if I did show my true colours, I doubt Wren would even like me.

Folding my arms across my chest, I look on with everyone else as Hayley runs through the routine. Except for faltering at the end of the last tumble, it looks like she's got it down pat. Leanne must agree, because she claps her hands once and says, "Okay, again, but this time with stunts. Grab your bases and back!"

By the time practice is finished I'm sweaty all over

and walking tenderly on my right foot. I landed on it the wrong way during my own tumble. I've had this tighter tumble routine I've been working on for weeks now, but can't seem to get it right. I start out with my legs longer, and after the third tumble I do a twist and a cartwheel. I'm supposed to finish the routine with four close-body tumbles — almost as if I'm staying in the same spot — and land on the mats in a front split with my head arched back. Whenever I do it, it starts out nicely and ends in a mess of arms and legs.

Some days I wonder if I still love cheer as much as I used to. Do I stick with it for *me*, or just because it's comfortable and another thing I do with my friends?

I'm walking to the change rooms with Hayley and Aiden when I hear Rain call my name. I consider ignoring them, but only because I'm not in the mood for Hayley's snobbish antics today. Rain's a good kid, and I'd prefer to keep them as far from Hayley's circle of judgment as I can.

"You going to group tonight?" Rain asks when they catch up to us. Rain is a year or so younger than us and on the cheer team, too. About six months ago, they started identifying as nonbinary, going by the pronouns they and their. Pansexual as well, I learned. I'm secretly happy they've come into themselves more the last little while, but unfortunately it was a change my homophobic friend witnessed.

"What group?" Hayley pushes open the doors to the change rooms, blocking Rain from following us in. She reaches up to pull the elastic out of her hair, ruffling loose the chestnut brown strands. "Until you admit you're a girl, Mallory, you're not changing in here with us."

I inwardly wince, wishing I had the courage to stand up to Hayley. But she and Aiden and the rest of our clique are all I have. I can't afford to lose friends I've had for years, even if I don't agree with everything they say or do. Dad walking out was enough for me to figure out I don't do well with change.

Rain scowls before tossing a look over their shoulder, probably to see if our coach is nearby. Leanne is at the other end of the gym, talking with our assistant coach, Chad. "Youth group," Rain finally supplies, glancing my way for confirmation.

I hold my breath, unsure of what to say and wishing I could disappear. Wishing Rain hadn't come so close to outing me and our youth group. Information like that is fuel for a power-hungry machine like Hayley. Now would be a great opportunity to officially come out of the closet, but when I open my mouth to agree, my evil twin makes herself present.

"*Why* are you talking to me right now? Eww."

Rain shrinks back when my friends laugh. The hurt on their face has my throat burning. The problem is, I can't seem to stop my hateful words from gushing out. "What does 'pansexual' even mean? Do you like … are you like attracted to different species, too?"

You don't have to say it. I already know. I'm a thieving, dishonest monster who would rather be *anything* but queer.

* * *

Have you ever found somewhere you know you can go and completely be yourself if you want to? Well, that motto is the entire billboard ad for youth group, and if I didn't have such thick armour, I'd be able to let my guard down more than just a teensy bit. Youth group is specifically organized for the LGBTQIA2S+ in the community, and it's kind of awesome to see how many misfits live in Charlottetown. We hang together, awkwardly bonding over bowling or movies or video games, and for an hour or two a week we can forget about the possibility of judgement or the exhaustion of figuring out who we are. I can stick one foot out of the closet while I'm here, and it's okay. The leaders are just glad I show up.

"Girl, what do you put in your hair to make it shine like that?"

I turn to see Daniel — or Dani, as he prefers to be called — plopping down in the empty seat beside me at the bowling alley. Once a month, the group facilitators rent out two lanes. We break into four groups, and the winners and losers of the first game play each other in the second. I glance across the table at Dani before lifting a hand to my hair. He has his own thick brown locks styled to one side of his head. The shaved undercut is dyed rainbow colours. How someone achieved that look is impressive.

I smile a little, pleased to offer him conditioning tips. "I use a shea butter serum. It removes the frizz, too."

"Oooh, I'll have to try it!" His eyes light up, and with blue eyeshadow and mascara he looks almost pretty. "I know it's not awful tonight, but you should see it in the summer. The humidity on this godforsaken island is saturated enough to ruin any queen's hair."

"I agree with you there." My name flashes on the bowling screen, indicating my turn has come. I tap my fingers on the table. "Be right back, Dani."

I'm not a great bowler. I'm not even a good one. If this were a school event, you wouldn't catch me dead up here making a fool of myself. But it's not, and though I suck so badly I land mostly gutter balls, I'm having a blast. I'm happy for once.

I scan the lineup, bypassing the many bland-coloured

bowling balls until I reach the navy blue one with orange swirls. While it's clearly not working, I deemed *this* one my good-luck charm months ago. I pick it up, moving closer to the starting point in my lane. Eyes are on me now, penetrating hawk-like ones watching, and not just the youth group members at my table.

Wren.

One name, one small, four-letter name, but with so much pack to it I immediately feel heavier. How am I supposed to roll this stupid ball down the lane with an audience? A short, frustratingly nervous breath leaves me when I pull back my arm. As soon as the ball takes off, I know it's a goner. Any time Wren is watching, my aim is off kilter.

Just like my mind, my heart, and everything else vulnerable.

Scowling, I head away from my lane and purposely seek out the lone emo in our group. Sitting at the other table one lane over, Wren's eyes briefly greet mine before slipping away again. For a person who stares at me like I'm some kind of celebrity, they sure can't hold their ground when the roles are reversed.

I don't stop at my table, instead marching directly to where Wren is seated. They're nursing a Dr. Pepper of all things, and looking everywhere but at me. People are watching us, but I don't care. I've never minded attention, and here at youth group I can talk to whoever I want.

"Hey. You've been staring at me all night." When they don't look at me, I snap my fingers in Wren's face. Standing this close, I can make out every piercing along their ear, the snake bites on each side of their bottom lip, their nose ring, and the small tattoo on their neck that they cover with hoodies at school. It's a sun with a face that is crying blood-red tears.

When they finally face me again, their makeup has me suddenly swallowing. I know the tear stains drawn on their cheeks in an extension of their mascara are for show, but there's a tiny compassionate part hidden in me that wonders if Wren is sad on the inside, too.

"Why don't you talk to me, like a normal person?" I demand, pulling Wren's attention from my lips back to my eyes. "Are you still pissed over the movies prank last year?"

Wren's beautiful hazel eyes darken for a moment, as if me bringing our almost date night up is a trigger for them.

"Wren, you're up." Marcus, one of the leaders, pats them on the shoulder.

"Thanks."

That one word has me leaning closer, savouring Wren's honey-smooth voice, but it's useless. They barely glance my way again. As they walk away, the urge to reach for them is strong.

It's a good thing I'm disciplined.

03 A Set-Up

HAYLEY IS WAITING FOR ME at my locker Monday morning. She and Aiden have been my best friends since we met in grade seven. We even joined the All-Star Cheerleading team together. Lately, though, it feels almost like I'm growing out of her. She's just ... Hayley, you know? I'm not heartless, despite what people say about me, and the things she does to people hit me in all my soft spots. Especially when her pranks target the one person I'm too afraid to like.

"So," Hayley begins as I reach my locker. She steps back as I get working on the number combination, a low laugh emphasizing her theatrics. Her gossip comes with enough hand gestures and facial expressions that I wonder why she never tried out for the school play. She could have easily stolen the lead role. "Guess what's in the works for our homely queer emo?"

Wren — with their pale face and black eyeshadow and liner — comes to mind, and my chest tightens. "Oh," I start slowly, annoyed that Wren takes up even a fraction of my thoughts so early in the morning. I run through all the possibilities of what Hayley could do to Wren, and the long list that comes to mind has my stomach bottoming out.

"So, do I need to do the twenty-question thing, or are you gonna enlighten me?" I close my locker, and together we head toward our Housing class. She shares two of my classes, and Aiden shares one. Unfortunately, we aren't all together in any classes this semester, although, Ben is in quite a few. It's as if karma knows I'm in the closet and thoroughly enjoys torturing me my senior year.

"You're no fun," Hayley teases, looping her arm through mine. A path is created for us in the busy hall — a perk to being popular, and one I accepted a long time ago. There is never a moment when I'm not being watched, sought out, hit on. It's exhausting to constantly be in the spotlight, but being a social pariah like Wren is? That has to suck. I could never jeopardize what I have now and risk sinking to their level. Not even for the chance to see more of Wren's rare smiles.

We spot the senior class nerd, Becky, walking in the same direction. She's been doing homework for students since the first week of tenth grade. Most of the merch I steal, I either sell and give her the cash in exchange for an assignment, or I just give her the merch. Becky loves studying and spending money on whatever nerdy things she's into, so it's a win-win for us both.

Hayley cuts in front of her, effectively blocking her path, since Ben and Hayley's boyfriend appear out of nowhere. We have Becky surrounded, and although it wasn't my idea to intimidate her this morning, I'm already reaching for my purse.

Hayley sneers at the red-faced girl, no doubt getting a thrill watching her almost piss herself in fear. "You know that garbage persuasive essay due tomorrow? You're gonna write it for me. Got it? Have it emailed to me no later than eleven tonight." There is absolutely no arguing with Hayley, so we watch Becky nod her head so fast, it's a wonder it doesn't pop off from fake enthusiasm.

"Hey, Becky," I add, handing her the ten bucks I still owe for the Shakespeare assignment she'll be working on. It's not due for another month, but I know she's good for it. Hayley never pays, and it's another thing I can't stand about her lately. I'm bad, but not *that* much of an asshole.

Hayley tweaks Becky on the nose, not aggressively or anything. More like a condescending love tap just to remind Becky who's boss. And then we're off again, sauntering down the halls like we own the place. Our boyfriends walk on either side of Hayley and me, acting as a silent force of overbearing muscle and yesterday's B.O.

Yay for me.

"*Anyway*, since you never guessed about the tricks up my sleeve, I'll let you enjoy the surprise when you find out," Hayley whispers as we enter the class. I take my usual seat in the back beside Ben. Hayley sits down between me and Adam. I don't get a chance to ask what she means because the teacher begins the lecture. It's not until break and we're heading to second period that I understand.

Jenna, one of Aiden's teammates from basketball, has Wren cornered in the hall. Jenna's posse of friends are there as well, although by the shuttered expression on Wren's face they're unnecessary. The rumours of what Wren has or hasn't done in their old school are a highlight of conversation some days, but being pressed against the locker right now has them looking anything but scary. I instantly feel bad, but as we come to a stop a few feet away, I freeze.

"My friend is into your whole ..." Jenna's voice trails off and she gestures to, well, *all* of Wren. I know Jenna is making this up, but it doesn't stop the jealousy flaring. Jealousy over someone liking Wren? "Goth look. She wants to ask you out but says something's been bugging her."

"Really. And what's that?" Wren answers Jenna, but as if they've sensed me in the hallway watching, they turn to catch my eye. Pressing my lips together, my heart starts to pound like I've just finished an hour of tumbling.

Jenna is grinning, drawing out the punchline. There are enough people in the hallway now to make a scene, and I have no doubt it's what she's waiting for. When she notices Wren's attention on me and not her, Jenna raises her voice. "Did you attack someone at your last school? Is that why you were expelled? She heard you bit them with your fangs and then licked up the blood."

The rumour is exaggerated, used for the sole purpose of hurting Wren. I expect them to walk away, push out of the circle around them, but a low chuckle rumbles from the back of Wren's throat. A dangerous smile appears, and my pulse quickens at how swiftly Wren's entire demeanour changes. Several people back away, including me.

"Do you see any fangs?" Wren asks, stepping closer and opening their mouth wide for Jenna.

Jenna screams.

Before I know it, security is there to grab Wren's shoulders, knocking books out of their arms. I watch in silent acceptance as papers sail to Wren's feet, not doing anything to help. I want to, but it's as if my feet are glued to the floor. One of their drawings flittering across the floor catches my attention.

"They were going to bite me!" Jenna accuses.

"Was not." Wren struggles against the man's grip.

"It's true." Hayley speaks up from beside me for the first time. I shift my focus and to see her eyes widening for obvious flair. When she holds a small knife out for the security to take, I actually hear my breath catch. *What the hell? Where did that come from?* "This fell out of Wren's jacket. Poor Jenna could have been seriously hurt if you hadn't stepped in."

"What? That's not mine!" Wren's gaze locks with mine once again, their voice thick from panic. "Please, *tell* them."

For a fraction of a second, I seriously consider speaking up. But then I remember who I am, and who Wren is. Being us sucks some days.

I turn away, resigning Wren to their fate.

* * *

"Why did you say there was a knife when there wasn't?" I ask later over burgers and milkshakes at DQ. I'm fuming. I've been trying to figure out all afternoon why Hayley would want Wren expelled. It seems her prejudice knows no bounds.

"Who cares? I wouldn't be surprised if the police were brought in. Who brings a knife to school, anyway? A freak, that's who." Ben grins at himself like he's the wittiest person at the table and high-fives Dylan and Adam. I roll my eyes. Ben's question is one I've thought of several times over the last few hours. Who brought in the knife? Had Hayley really picked it up off the floor and I didn't notice? Or had she had it in her pocket the entire time?

"Okay, one more. I was blinking the last time."

As if I hadn't even spoken, Hayley and Aiden cozy up for another selfie. I sigh, picking absentmindedly at my cheeseburger, and look out the restaurant window. I'm not overly hungry today, and it's unlike me to let Hayley's actions bother me. Maybe it's *my* actions I can't let go of. I should have said something, but I didn't. Maybe Wren getting in trouble was a result of me being a silent bystander.

"There could have been a knife, though, right? We saw how fast Wren went at Jenna," Aiden supplied after a moment. She picked up her milkshake, shrugging. "I'm just saying. I could totes see them attacking someone at their old school."

"That's just a rumour," Dylan and I say at the same time, and I watch him drape his arm across Aiden's shoulder. They've been a couple all through high school. It's hard not to be a little jealous over anyone who knows what they want in love and life. Dylan and Aiden are such goals.

Wren's face comes to mind, stirring a strange

flutter in the pit of my stomach. Lately, being their focus has me all confused and I'm left feeling things I've never felt the entire time I've been with Ben. I *like* Wren's attention, and I hate that about myself. Why can't I get all tingly whenever Ben looks at me?

"My question is, does anyone know why the psycho wears their eyeliner that low? They can't honestly think it makes them look cool?" Hayley scoffs at that idea, reaching across for one of Adam's fries. She thanks him with a kiss, one that lingers far too long for an audience.

I cut my eyes to my phone, needing a distraction of something besides my best friend playing tonsil hockey. Wren's drawing that had fallen on the floor earlier fills my lock screen, and I smile a little. When I saw the manga drawing of what must be one of their favourite characters, I couldn't believe how good it was. I thought of taking it home, but I took a picture instead before slipping it back into Wren's locker. I surprise even myself some days. I don't know what it is, but something about Wren makes me think twice on a lot of things.

The subject of Wren is dropped a few minutes later, and we drive back to school for afternoon classes. I spend way too much time in Biology trying to hear gossip about the standoff in the hall, and between third and fourth period I don't spot Wren anywhere. It's not until I'm shopping with Hayley after school that she informs me they were suspended.

"I heard the principal watched the security cameras but couldn't figure out where the knife came from," she gleefully tells me. I start wondering how long she and Jenna had planned to gang up on Wren. "The guard totes bought my story. I should be an actress, right?"

I give her a slow nod, my mind elsewhere as I scan the natural supplements. I feel terrible, and can't express how unusual that is for me. Just last year I was asking Wren to the movies on a dare and standing them up. Now I'm genuinely concerned for them.

"What are you looking for, anyway?"

"I saw an ad for this new low-carb protein powder I want to try and figured if anyone sold it, it'd be Shoppers," I explain, spotting the brand on the top shelf. A sudden urge to boost my All-Star flyer friend up to grab it has me stifling a laugh, but I'm angry with Hayley. I wouldn't want to help her in the thrill department with the way she's been acting, and so I resist.

"I don't see it. Let's just go."

"Okay, but one more thing," Hayley murmurs, pulling her gaze from the shelf to look at me. She grins, and evil is the only word that comes to mind to describe it. "See the green tea fat-burner supplements? I want you to steal them for me."

Sometimes, I wish I could say no to her. I really do.

04 Own Worst Enemy

WHAT HAPPENED TO WREN nags at me for the rest of the week, and I don't appreciate or need the newfound compassionate side of me. It's weak, and if I'm not careful, Hayley will turn on me, too. I must be crazy to let a nobody like Wren take my mind hostage and risk ruining everything I've spent the last several years building. I can't be queer and still have my friends, so the Wren-obsessed thoughts have gotta quit.

Uh-huh. Tell *that* to the bleeding heart who

secretly doodles *W* into all their notebooks like some kind of lovesick My Chemical Romance fan.

By the time Sunday evening rolls around, I'm standing outside the entrance of youth group. Waiting, and clearly a sucker for nerds. It's cold, and as I greet Dani and Rain heading into the building, I'm burrowed as far as I can go inside my winter coat. I haven't seen Wren since their suspension, and after fifteen minutes I'm half convinced they won't show tonight.

This is stupid.

I'm about to pull open the door and go in when I finally see them casually strolling up the walkway. With a cigarette dangling from their bare fingertips inside cut-off gloves, it's quite a fashion statement in minus-fifteen weather. "Wren, hey," I manage. Standing in front of them now, all the speeches I practised earlier are lost to me.

Wren doesn't acknowledge me right away, which is a first. They lift the cigarette to their lips, taking a long drag before tossing the butt in the snowbank. A gust of cool air leaves their parted lips as they exhale the smoke out. "I don't know what game you're playing," Wren says slowly, reaching for the door as well.

Our fingers almost touch, but I don't pull away. A rush of heat warms my chilled cheeks at being so close to Wren and I stammer, "No game this time. I just … want to say I'm sorry. For last week. You didn't … I know that wasn't your knife."

Jeez, I sound like a fumbling idiot.

"Whatever." Wren shrugs, a bored look on their face.

I frown, not knowing what to say to that. Their obvious indifference is a complete 180, but it's the disinterest in Wren's eyes that steals my breath. For the first time in my life, I don't know what step to take. I'm struggling, at a loss for words. But for once, Wren has plenty.

"Don't bother, Tage. I thought you might be different, but you're not. You're no better than Hannah, or Hayley, or whatever her name is. You can all go to hell for all I care."

* * *

I wasn't always like this.

My dad and I used to be super close before he went away. He'd come to all my cheer practices and help me build science projects and race me to the top of the water slide at Shining Waters. I was a good kid, and for the most part, a good teenager. I would talk to him about everything — school, friends, boys (eye roll). When he told me I should feel comfortable telling him anything, I believed him. It turns out, there were some things he couldn't deal with, and the huge crush I had on Amber from my cheer team was one of them.

I'll never forget that day. I was helping him with the dishes after supper. Mom was setting up a board game, a rare night off to spend with us. I remember the nervous butterflies as I thought of the exact words I wanted to say, the perfect angle I'd use to come out to him. When it happened ten minutes later — halfway between naming my crush and admitting to someone other than my cat Bruno that I was queer — he was washing the largest knife from our butcher's block. He must have been distracted because he cut himself pretty badly and had to go to the

ER. My confession was pushed to the back burner, and we never talked about it again. Gone were the heart-to-hearts between my dad and me. Our relationship became awkward and forced. I could tell there were things he wanted to talk about, but never had the courage to. And when he moved away, I guess he took the best parts of me with him.

Ever since Wren gave me the cold shoulder at youth group on Sunday, I've been a supreme bitch. Call it hormones, insecurity, denial, whatever the hell you want to, but know this: I've declared open season on anyone at school who looks at me without the utmost respect plastered on their face. And that goes for Wren. *Especially* Wren.

Because I can't *stand* how I let them in enough to hurt me.

"You're in my seat," I announce at the beginning of Art class Tuesday morning, scowling down at Wren and fully expecting them to move. We have an audience, but I didn't account for Wren's reaction — or *non-reaction*, I should say. They're hunched over their desk, fingers inside cut-off gloves rapidly sketching a portrait of someone, a woman. I can tell from the soft edging around the jawline.

"Look again. Don't you sit in the back, with the other 'cool' kids?"

Wren's low voice has a couple people around us giggling, and I snap my fingers to direct the attention back to me. We only have a few minutes before Ms. Thompson shows up to start the class. "Hey, look at me."

Hayley chuckles from her seat at the back. "Ooh, I'm liking this Tage."

Wren doesn't straighten up to face me, and my only guess is they're throwing a big figurative 'F you' my way. I used to feel them watching me all the time, but since their suspension Wren has been openly angry at me. Their rejection at youth group when I tried to apologize stung, but their cocky disregard for me right now has me pulling their toque off. When they twist in their seat to grab it, I reach around to snatch their sketchbook off the desk. The drawing is exceptional, almost lifelike. Wren's skill is unmatched in this class, and I'm not the only one who has noticed. Jenna remarks all the time how Wren's the teacher's pet.

"Tage, stop it, *please.*"

It's as if I'm underwater, though. Wren's hushed pleas sound muffled in the distance, and I tear the portrait out before I can stop myself. "Who is this you're drawing? Your girlfriend?" My laugh is forced, but if I'm set on becoming Hayley this week, mocking laughter is a must. I wave the drawing around, showing Wren's impeccable talent off to the class. The woman in the picture is beautiful, sitting on a park bench overlooking the wharf. Something about her is familiar, but I can't figure it out right off the bat. I dodge Wren's grab at the drawing.

"I don't know, she looks too hot to be Wren's girl."

"Too old."

"She's not emo enough. Wren needs someone to play dress up, too." That remark comes from Jenna, who for some reason has her own agenda when it comes to Wren. I watch as she laughs, her braces flashing in the process. I feel a rush of bitterness at the thought of

Jenna volunteering for such a role, and I turn to glare at Wren again.

They're standing before me now, books and bag in their arms like admitting defeat is a possibility. For a millisecond, something powerful passes between us, and I have to catch my breath. Wren is watching me intently, the green flecks in their light brown eyes more pronounced with the thick rim of eyeliner and blood-red eyeshadow. It would create a heart-wrenching image in front of my camera lens. Photography and sculpture are why I chose Art class the last two years. Jenna and Hayley just followed suit.

"Please, Tage. I don't know what you're dealing with, but taking it out on me won't fix it."

Wren's voice sweeps over me, breaking whatever heart-pounding spell they had me wrapped up in. The sound of my name coming from their lips has me all kinds of messed up, and when I blink, my gaze drops down to the drawing.

"Let me see it," Hayley demands, beside me now. She swipes the portrait out of my hands, giving it a once over before clicking her tongue. "Yup, I bet that's the freak's mommy. My brother's friends with Wren's."

My mouth feels like cotton balls, it's so dry. The beautiful woman in the drawing catches my gaze again, and I struggle to swallow. *What happened to Wren's mom?*

Wren gasps as Hayley rips the drawing down the middle with a smirk. She's silent as she hands the remains back to Wren, finishing her act with a small bow.

"Hayley," I say uncertainly.

She chuckles, her eyes glimmering with mischief. As she heads back to her seat, she calls over her shoulder, "You're welcome, honey."

My gaze collides with Wren's, and my heart immediately squeezes at the shuttered expression clouding their face. Whoever it was in the picture, she was someone important. Like everything, I've stolen it away. I thought Wren hating me would be a lot easier to deal with than *my* complicated feelings for *them*.

I couldn't be any more wrong.

05 The Snowstorm

ANOTHER CHEER PRACTICE, another party, another awkward conversation with Mom as we rush through the week's mornings. Seven more days of hiding who I am and slowly dying inside.

Every touch of Ben's hands, the soft but masculine feel of his lips on mine, his boyish immaturity ... *I can't take it anymore.*

"What's wrong? You're not even watching," Ben's lips brush my ear as he whispers.

My entire body goes rigid, unmoving. For a moment all the air in the movie theatre evaporates, and my mouth flaps open like a fish as I try to catch my breath. Ben's presence is too much.

"I can't do this with you." The words fly from my mouth in a jumbled rush, and I'm jumping to my feet before I know what I'm doing.

Ben huffs a laugh, glancing at our friends on either side of us before settling on me again. "Do what? C'mon, Tage, you're causing a scene."

"What's wrong?" Hayley asks, leaning around Adam to look at me.

"Are you sick? I can …"

I've got a golf ball-sized lump in my throat, and the ringing in my ears drowns out whatever else Ben is saying. Aiden reaches for my hand, but I pull away from her, too, bending to gather my purse and jacket. "I'm done, Ben," I rasp. "I … I can't be your girlfriend. I can't be your anything."

I rush down the theatre stairs and through the exit, batting tears away as I struggle to put on my coat.

Public break-ups aren't my thing, but I'm not thinking straight and if Ben had moved in to touch me one more time I might have lost my supper in his lap.

"Tage, wait up! Please."

I hear Ben before I see him, and briefly wonder if I can pretend I didn't and just leave. My hand is on the door when he stops me, shoving his body between me and the exit. He doesn't try to touch me again, and for that I'm grateful.

"Why are we breaking up again? I can't figure you out, and it's damn tiring."

I grip my purse closer, needing comfort and not having anyone I want to hold on to. When I sniffle, Ben's sorrowful gaze meets mine. His pain matters to me, and I hate how I've strung him along for so long. I open my mouth to tell him everything, but when I see Hayley and Aiden behind him, another half truth slips out. "This is our last break-up, I swear. I'm sorry. It's not you, it's me."

It's always me.

* * *

Dramatic relationship endings are only as effective as the planned exit.

PEI in the middle of winter is *not* a great time to plan a break-up and leave by car, just as an FYI. I'm still sitting in the parking lot twenty minutes later, watching the rapid swipe of my wipers as they clear the heavy snowflakes from my windshield. In the hour I was in the movie, a freaking snowstorm started. Apprehension about driving in dirty weather has my gut rolling worse than it was with Ben's touch. I haven't told anyone this, but it took me three times to pass my driver's test. I blame it mostly on my mom, since she insisted I take the test in the winter.

I chew the inside of my cheeks, unsure if I can even make it home in this. Stubborn determination has me refusing to wait for my friends to come to my rescue, but maybe … just maybe my mom can be my hero for once. This morning she said she had the night off, but I've checked my cell about fifty times since I left the movie, and she hasn't messaged me once. With almost zero visibility outside, if I ever thought having a cop for a mom would give me some nagging parental worry, I was sorely mistaken.

Because I'm stupid, and the idea of driving downtown has me sweating inside my winter coat, I ring Constable Fitzgerald anyway. Sucker for punishment and all that. Who knows? Maybe she's pacing the floors of our two-storey, trying not to be overprotective of me but secretly nervous I'm not home yet.

"Tage," Mom says after the fourth ring, my name tumbling past her lips in a rush. The sound of sirens in the background makes me slump in my seat. *So much for having the night off.* "Can't talk now. There's been a pile-up on the number one heading toward Mount Stewart. I'll be home late tonight, okay?"

"I'm actually not —" I begin, but dispatch coming through her cruiser's radio cuts me off.

"Love you, honey. Gotta go!"

I frown as Mom disconnects our call, holding my cell to my ear long after the screen goes dark. Once again, I'm in silence, staring ahead at the storm brewing past the windshield. "Stupid, stupid," I mutter, pulling the seatbelt across my body. The next time I break things off with someone, I'm doing myself a favour and checking the forecast first. Or better yet, I'll wait until summer, or do it at my house. Then they can be the one to awkwardly leave.

"Don't be such a baby," I scold myself, taking a deep breath and flicking on the headlights. I shift into drive, pressing lightly on the gas to ease the car forward. Instead of heading home Mount Edward Road way like I usually do after a movie date, I make my way slowly through the mall parking lot. Driving down North River Road would be an easy straight line, and I wouldn't have to go through any roundabouts or turn half a dozen times. With it storming, I'm not bothering with University Avenue either. It's too busy, and I'm the kind of girl who stops instead of yields when entering the roundabout and lets everyone else go first. Hayley and Ben tease me all the time over it. Apparently, once or twice I waited for someone leaving the Mount Edward Tim Hortons to enter the roundabout before me.

I don't *remember* doing that, so I take their stories as fiction until I'm proven otherwise.

I'm accelerating past the second stop sign in front of the main doors to the mall when a black, snow-covered hoodie catches my eye. I let my foot off the gas, squinting out my passenger window at the lone figure huddled inside the bus shelter. The snow is really coming down, and with the brutal wind chill there's no way a bus or cab will still be on the roads to pick the guy up.

My Camry coasts slowly to the corner, where I'll need to turn right and drive past them. Indecision has my foot hanging in limbo, halting me from pressing the gas or the brake. Whoever is in the shelter is a boob, totally underdressed for the storm they're caught up in. My eyes narrow as I watch them, trying to figure out who would be that small, stupid, and at a risk of frostbite. I'm legit concerned for them right now, but I don't think I want them in my car. Stranger danger is a real thing, and this guy looks like he's got nothing to lose.

What are you gonna do, let them freeze to death? Maybe you are like Hayley.

I pump the brakes hard, bringing the car to a stop. "Bullshit. Hayley is one bitch I am *not*." Not anymore.

Scrambling to unbuckle, I shove the driver's door open before I remember to put the car in park. "Hey!" I yell, waving my hands in the shelter's direction. "Need a drive?" The guy has his back to me, and I'm halfway to the glass shelter when I realize I left my perfectly warmed car several feet away. My heart is beating too fast to be normal, and I figure, if I get killed tonight, the joke is definitely on me. Like, how close do I need to get for them to hear me?

I'm a car length away when the guy notices me frantically waving. "Finally!" I exclaim, salty as hell for no other reason than the shitty situation I'm currently in. I glower at them, my stomach fluttering at the fact their face is hidden from the baggy hoodie. "You want a lift?"

They reach up, pulling their hoodie and headphones off, and my mouth hits my chest when Wren's pissed-off face comes into view.

Something between a laugh and a shout bubbles to the surface as a gush of relief and worry takes over. "Wren, ohmygod. What the hell are you doing out in this?"

Snow covers the back of their jeans, like they'd fallen in their search for shelter, and it makes the already tight fabric look damp and stiff. Flurries gusting into the open structure sprinkle onto Wren's face, melting off their sharp nose, prominent chin. I itch to brush the wetness it leaves behind, and the impulsive thought has me kicking myself.

"What are *you* doing out in this?" Wren finally mutters, pulling my attention from their lips back up to the shadows in their eyes.

I huff, not having the patience for a standoff. "Let me drive you home, Wren, please. It's way too cold tonight." Wren doesn't trust me, which makes sense considering it was only a few days ago I stood by and watched Hayley destroy a beautifully illustrated portrait of theirs.

Wren stiffens, their gaze shifting to my car still idling on the corner in front of the mall. "I'll take my chances."

Wren's hushed voice guts me like the sharpest knife, and I'm left exposed, the chill of the winter storm seeping into raw wounds. Disgrace for everything I've done is an acid to my steel armour, melting through my layers until it's all I can do not to collapse where I stand. Am I so horrible, Wren would rather face frostbite than get in the car with me? I spin away, not waiting to hear if they've changed their mind, and stomp back to my car.

Please come, please don't be stupid, Wren. I'm sorry.

I'm taking a chance, but already a plan B is formulating. If Wren won't come to me, then I'll camp out beside them until they come to their senses. Wren doesn't strike me as the type to let another person suffer, no matter how hurt they've made them.

"You're seriously gonna just walk away?" Wren demands from behind me, but they sound a lot closer than where I left them. "Such a Tage thing to do, turning your back — whoa!"

I turn just as Wren's wiry frame crashes into me. Reflex has me grabbing for them, trying to keep us upright, but my feet have other plans. My Uggs skid back and forth on the ice with Wren, and for a hot second I want to laugh at how ridiculous we must look. Just like a scene from a movie, I feel the moment my Uggs leave the ground, and I make a mad grab for Wren. My fingers hook into the straps of their backpack, but all it does it take them with me. They land on top of me in the middle of the parking lot, the frozen material of their hood pressed into my face. I groan, wishing I'd landed on a thick blanket of a cheer mat instead of snow. The back of my head throbs in a dull ache.

"Tage, you okay?" Wren scrambles off me, and seconds later I'm staring up into those intoxicating, now worried eyes.

"Yeah. You?"

Wren's guarded expression returns, almost like they momentarily forgot they're supposed to be mad. "Yup." The word rolls off their tongue with an exaggerated pop toward the end, finishing the sarcasm off with a scowl aimed at me.

"I wasn't going to leave you," I insist, pushing up off the ground as well. I brush the snow off my clothes, feeling an ache begin in my back from the fall.

"Sure looked that way."

Sighing, I trudge back to my Camry, calling over my shoulder, "Get in the car, Wren." Because I'm hella impulsive and left the driver's door gaping open, there is quite a buildup of snow on the seat I have to brush off before getting in.

Wren opens the passenger door, a small smirk teasing the corners of their mouth as they get in. "You didn't think that one through, did you."

I grimace but don't give in to the temptation of replying. I'm tired and have officially frozen my ass off. Fortunately, having the car idle kept most of the snow from building up on the windshield. When I check my blind spots and mirrors and lurch forward once more, I do say one thing. "Wren, I would never have left you out in the cold." I shoot a quick glance to my passenger, not missing the way those pretty hazel eyes narrow. I reach across the car's console, touching their arm gently. "I promise, okay? I was just going to move the car. I'd planned to sit outside with you 'til you came to your senses."

06 Confessions in the Night

TONIGHT HASN'T TURNED OUT at all like I planned, but even if my head is reluctant, my heart is all for the direction it's taken.

Sharing curious looks with Wren at school and creeping their moody pics on social doesn't come close to what I'm doing now. As we stand in socked feet just inside Wren's parents' living room, the bundle of nerves coming off them has me guessing Wren is in the same boat.

"Uh, Pops, this is Tage. A … friend from school."

Wren's dad is seated on the floor, pieces of a brand-new bookcase scattered around him. The empty IKEA box rests on the sofa behind him. He hardly looks at us, just grunts a burly hello as he picks up the nearby tool. Invisible aggression drips off him, saturating the room, so much that I'm the one grabbing Wren's arm to pull us away.

"Is he going to be okay with me staying the night?" I blurt when we're alone in Wren's room with the door closed.

Wren nods, licking their lips. "Michele will make sure of it. She's good, she's —"

"Where?"

"Her office, in the basement," Wren explains. "She does bookkeeping as a side job from the bank."

"And she's your stepmom?"

"Yep."

Wren moves into the room more, heading to the closet. As they swap out their wet hoodie for a dry one, I busy myself by scanning the decor on the walls.

Posters of favourite bands take one entire wall hostage, and the rest of the walls and window frames are covered in punk-related merch and several sketches. I spot the various chains and symbols similar to Wren's tattoo draped over the ends of the curtain rods.

"Very emo of you," I muse, darting a quick glance in Wren's direction. Their wry grin has girly butterflies going wild in the pit of my stomach again. Heat floods my cheeks, and I turn back to the sketches. I spot a familiar drawing taped to the wall beside Wren's desk and guilt has me clearing my throat. I reach for the drawing, trailing fingers lightly over the woman's face.

"My mom," Wren confirms from beside me. I hadn't heard them move across the room, and now they're taking my space as their own. I suck in a nervous breath when Wren's fingers brush my hand, also touching the woman's face. "She died when I was only three."

Our eyes meet, and without the charade of school I find I'm greedily soaking them in. My gaze roams over tousled, purposely messy black hair that for once isn't occupied with a toque, to dark makeup around intelligent hazel eyes.

"I'm sorry Hayley tore it up. It's really a beautiful drawing," I whisper, my attention landing on Wren's mouth. I've wasted so much time kissing Ben the last two years. I don't know where my fascination stems from, but I'd really like to kiss Wren.

"I'll uh …" Wren coughs a little, dropping their hand and turning away from me. "I'll find you something to wear. I imagine the storm will be over in the morning and you can go home."

"Thanks. I appreciate you letting me crash here."

Wren nods, pulling open the bedroom door. Wariness at me being here is so clear on their face it makes me ache in places I thought dead long ago. They don't trust me, don't trust that I won't hurt them more than I've done already. "I'm gonna grab a sleeping bag. Don't steal anything while I'm gone."

My eyebrows shoot up at Wren's flippant comment. Do they know me so well to assume the thought of lifting something might cross my mind? Taking a closer look at Wren's things, specifically their chains and brand-new pair of Converse resting just inside their closet, I don't have my usual restless need to steal. I'm not a kleptomaniac, I can control my thieving ways. Most of the time I just don't want to.

"How's the head?" Wren asks when they return five minutes later with pillows, a sleeping bag, and blanket.

"Better, thanks." I watch as they make a bed for me on the floor next to theirs. The room isn't very big, so it's really the only place that won't block the door.

"What angle are you playing at, Tage?" Wren suddenly asks, a deep frown setting their mouth in a hard line. They head to the dresser, pulling open the second drawer and rummaging for a moment before tossing me a set of pajamas. "It was only a week ago you pulled that stunt in class. Do you hate me so much you'd lead me on, have me falling for you? Again?"

"I *don't* hate you. That's the problem," I reluctantly admit, giving Wren a sad smile. I shrug, breaking their stare and glance down to the clothes in my arms. "I like you, always have. It's *me* I hate. You've always been so confident with who you are, and I've been hiding who …" My voice trails off. Even now, I struggle with the truth. Out of everyone I know, Wren should be the easiest to confide in.

"Who you are?" Wren finally deadpans. The room is so quiet that even the faint swishing of Wren's damp denims as they cross the room sound like percussion cymbals. Seconds later they're cupping my chin between their thumb and index finger, tilting my face up to greet theirs. "For the record, you never needed to hide from me. What you *needed* to do was ditch Hayley."

Wren releases their grip, and a soft gasp escapes me at the sudden loss. My gaze drops down, marvelling over how right it feels to be here with Wren. Even when I've hurt them and they're distrustful. Wanting to make them understand a side of me no one has bridged before, I'm the one to reach out this time. I slip my hand in Wren's, linking our fingers together, pleased when they don't automatically pull away. Their black nail polish matches my indigo blue nails perfectly. "You're *exactly* who I should hide from."

God, my voice is way huskier than intended, and my cheeks flush hot as I pull away from Wren. By the hurt in their eyes, and the hard set to their chin, I get the feeling I'm the only one who took my words as a compliment. "I don't … I'm not out at all at school, Wren, and I've been hiding for so long. If anyone knew the real me, o—or knew I was looking at you? It's too risky."

Tension is thick in the air, and after a long minute of observing the hard ridge of Wren's set jawline, I realize a quick explanation won't be enough to repair the damage between us. Not knowing what else to say tonight, I gesture to the pajamas tucked under my arm in a football hold. "I'll uh …" I lick my lips and try again. "I'll get changed. Is the bathroom down the hall?"

"Just change here. I'll leave, I … need air anyway." Frowning, I watch Wren rifle through their dresser once more before leaving me alone again.

Guess the overdue pee break will have to wait.

I flump down on the corner of Wren's bed, a heavy sigh relaxing my shoulders, and for about the tenth time tonight I wonder where my usual attitude disappeared to. At school I'd never let anyone get the upper hand, but in Wren's domain I'm all but speechless. I consider the possible reasons as I get into the red shirt and plaid bottoms, grateful for Wren's earlier thoughtfulness.

After waiting another few minutes for Wren, I pull my cell out of my jeans pocket before dropping the clothes I'd worn beside the makeshift bed. Scrolling through the missed messages, I grimace when I notice the few snaps from Aiden. She's a good friend, wondering what happened with me earlier. There's a text from Mom, making sure I lock the doors when I go to bed. Bitterness cuts in on my good mood, and I delete her message without replying. I shoot a quick snap back to Aiden.

Tage: idk … Bring you up to speed tmr.

It's late, almost one in the morning, but within a minute I get a reply.

Aiden: r u ok tho, SRSLY?

I hesitate. I'm dying to fill her in, but apprehension holds me back on the off chance she's more like Hayley than I realize. Aiden's never come across as openly prejudiced, but that's the thing about followers. They're a lot like chameleons, willing to adapt to anything for survival. Putting blind faith in the wrong people and not trusting anyone is kind of my thing, so I know whatever I tell Aiden, Hayley will probably hear by Monday.

Tage: Yes, fine. Have a good night.

I'm tucking my phone under my pillow when Wren knocks on the bedroom door. "You decent?"

"If you mean dressed, then yes." My response has a bit more bite to it, a bit more defensive Tage, and I welcome the intrusion. Laying myself out for Wren is a risk I'll likely never be comfortable taking. Stealing has the same rush but without the aftershocks of heartbreak.

Slipping inside the sleeping bag, I'm aware of Wren looking everywhere but at me when they come in. Avoidance is what I should be doing, too, but curiosity of what Wren looks like all ready for bed has my eyes trained on them as they move around the room. "Wow. You look so … different."

Seriously? Is *not* flirting with Wren even an option anymore?

"Uh-huh."

They turn on their bedside lamp before walking back to the door to flick off the light, not giving me any more than that. The MCR t-shirt and bottoms they're wearing are whatever, you know, typical gender-neutral pajamas. It's the lack of makeup that has me staring with my mouth legit hanging open as they climb under the covers. Their face is a shade darker without the foundation, effectively taking the chill out of their hazel eyes. I don't know why, but Wren sleeping with their makeup on seemed more likely to me. Gone is the tough outer shell Wren faces each day with, and in its place is …

"You're beautiful."

The words are out before I have a chance to examine them, and my eyes widen as Wren visibly tenses. "I mean handsome. Or cute? Help me out here, Wren. I … is there a right word you feel more comfortable with?"

Is there a right way to keep from humiliating us both?

"All of the above is fine." Wren turns on their side away from me, halting any other conversation. "'Night, Tage."

"Goodnight."

Uncomfortable silence descends on the dimly lit room, and for a long time I study Wren's still form. I only know two people who identify as nonbinary, yet even when I'm trying to be respectful, I still manage to offend them. I'm not sure which part of what I said upset Wren, but unintentionally hurting them more nags at me.

"Wren?"

Wren's drawn-out sigh echoes off the walls of the room, sounding a lot louder than it probably is, and a moment later the bedsprings groan as they turn over to face me. "Don't you sleep?"

I bite my lip, facing off with them and for an unsteady heartbeat or three we stare at each other. "Does it bother you that I think you're cute?"

Wren shakes their head, their gaze roaming over

my face. The shoulder they're not lying on goes up in a shrug. "You like how I look now, but it's the version I hate the most."

An unwelcome ache settles in my chest. Just as it had earlier, a strange urge to be honest has me scooting closer to the bed. I reach for Wren, giving them plenty of time to pull away before ghosting my hand across their smooth cheek. Wren's gaze widens seconds before their entire body is melting into my touch, those same eyes fluttering closed. I trace Wren's bottom lip, sliding over their piercings and fascinated by the quiver I feel under my thumb.

"Sorry if what I said sounded like a new realization when it comes to you, but what makes you think I don't find you beautiful, or handsome, or cute at school?"

07 Butterflies and Smiles

THE NEXT MORNING, I wake up on my side with Wren's hand still curled into mine from the night before. Memories of us talking until well after 4:00 a.m. are still fresh, and I smile sleepily. Once I'd given in to feeling something for Wren and letting my armour slip, finding things to talk about had been as natural as breathing. Even for Wren, it seemed, who hardly ever talked to anyone — not just me.

I observe them now, not quite ready to pull my

hand away and create any sort of distance between us. Wren is sound asleep on their stomach, arm hanging off the bed and fingers hooked in mine. The short sleeve of the t-shirt they're wearing rides up, and I get a peek at another small tattoo, this time in a design of a barcode. It sits just above the elbow, acting as a starting point to a map of faint, horizontal lines toward Wren's bicep. My smile slips as I narrow my eyes, squinting to get a closer look. The lines are etched into Wren's skin, thin slivers zigzagging from their elbow to armpit, and a sinking feeling weighs heavily on me.

I swallow past the lump now in my throat, carefully getting to my feet so I don't wake Wren. Surely those scars aren't what I think they are, right? Wren's emo, but not *that* emo. Right? That has to be a thing, because contemplating reasons they might have been cutting all leads back to me. Me and Hayley. Rebellious tears prick my eyes, and I look away from Wren to the window across their bedroom. By the view of the front yard, the storm is still going full throttle. All the blowing has caused huge drifts to pile against the house and the middle of the street, making driving anytime soon a no-go for this girl. Rather than focus on the million-to-one chance I have at becoming Wren's girl, I choose optimism. If we're going to be near one another today, then the most I should hope for is gaining Wren's trust. And friendship.

A small grin claims my mouth, and as I silently make my way to the bathroom there's a light bounce to my step. I pee and wash my hands and face before finger-combing my ash blond hair, wanting to look my best for my broody emo crush. Just because the odds are against me, it doesn't mean I won't come prepared for anything.

"*What* has gotten into you?" I mutter, biting my lip as a burst of excited jitters make me nauseous. I check my teeth in the mirror, noting the after-sleep film over them and wrinkle my nose. I wish I had my toothbrush, or at least thought to ask Wren for one the night before. Morning breath won't cut it if I have any hopes of getting closer to Wren.

To talk, remember?? Skank.

Snickering at my internal scolding, my gaze falls to the vanity drawers under the sink. I cock my head toward the door, listening for anyone nearing the bathroom. When silence answers, I bend and carefully slide open each drawer until I come across a couple spare toothbrushes still in packaging. My fingers stab into the backing, prying the brush out slowly so it doesn't make all the loud crinkling. Technically, I'm snooping *and* stealing, but it's just a two-dollar toothbrush. Wren would have given me one had I asked.

I bump into Wren's stepmother as I leave the bathroom, and as Michele grabs my arms to hold me upright, my minty breath so close has guilt gnawing at me. I'm *never* guilty about stealing. "Morning! Did you sleep okay? Had Wren given me a heads-up one of their friends would be storm-stayed here, I would have dug out the air mattress from storage."

I smile, already liking Michele ten times more than the first impression I got of Wren's father. I recognize her from the downtown bank, and know she works in one of the back offices. A mortgage specialist or something, I think. "The floor was fine, Mrs. McMillan. Thanks for letting me stay."

She waves my gratitude away. "Please call me Michele. I sound old whenever people call me Mrs." We walk down the hall together, stopping outside Wren's door. Michele smiles. "I'll make a batch of pancakes and bacon in a little bit. Wren's a heavy sleeper, but feel free to grab a shower or come chat with me. I doubt you'll be going anywhere this morning."

"Thank you, Mrs. ... I mean, Michele," I reply, smiling and practically swooning over her maternal instincts. Hell, maybe I can move in here permanently. How long would it take for Mother Dearest to notice?

When I come back in the room, the smile tugging at Wren's mouth as they dream stops me in my tracks. That one innocent smile has my heart skipping beats like nothing but cheerleading, with its strenuous routines and never-ending tumbles, ever could. Wanting to capture it for later, I grab my phone to snap a few pictures. Turns out Wren isn't as heavy a sleeper as Michele had suggested, because they wake up at the sound.

"The hell are you doing?" Wren jolts out of the bed, looking adorably sleepy yet catastrophically pissed off. The death glare piercing me as they rip the phone from my hands makes me shrink back. "What were you planning to do, snap my picture to all your friends?"

"No! No, Wren, I wasn't, I swear. That's not it at all."

Wren's hands are trembling as they try to unlock my phone, muttering curses every time a code doesn't work. I can tell they're not really listening to me. A tightness in my chest steals my breath as a lone tear splashes on Wren's cheek. "I'll delete it if you want."

Wren nods, their actions jerky as they shove the phone back into my hands. Pain-filled hazel eyes glistening with unshed tears bore into me before Wren stares over my shoulder. "Yeah, I *want*. I don't trust you. Not after the last time. How do I know Hayley won't get hold of the picture and draw homophobic slurs on my face before it goes viral? The last time I trusted you I had to pick popcorn out of my hair and hoodie for *hours*."

Nodding in understanding, my own vision is blurry with tears as I unlock my phone. The prank I took part in the year before. Everything with Wren came back to that night, spoiling whatever was in its path like a bad taste in my mouth. I'd go back in time if I could, alter the chain of events to ease Wren's life a little more. There is so much I'd do, starting with a real date. There hasn't been a day since the prank that I haven't felt shame over the fake one I set Wren up on.

Half the school knew they liked me, and when my friends put me up to it, I thought it'd be a good chance to kill the crush Wren had on me. They had no idea I'd stand them up at the last minute to our movie date. In my defence, I'd hoped Wren wouldn't be the type to sit through a movie alone and would just head home after I bailed. My luck sucks, though, and not only did Wren see me waltz into the theatre with all my friends that night, I also had to grin and bear it when Hayley positioned us in the row directly behind them. Just for *thinking* Wren had a chance with me, Hayley made us all throw popcorn at them until they couldn't take it anymore. I'll never forget the hurt look Wren gave me seconds before running out of the theatre.

My throat aches at the memory, and when I gulp, the time I swallowed a glob of natural peanut butter comes to mind, the lump scratching its way down to the pit of my stomach. A traitorous tear slips out, and then another, and then we're both standing in the middle of Wren's bedroom, crying like fools. Accessing the pictures I'd taken, I'm half blind from the tears when I offer my phone to Wren. "I just wanted to capture how perfect you are, so when I'm home I can think about being here. With you. I am … God, I'm so sorry for what I did to you, Wren." My bottom lip quivers, and, unable to hold Wren's gaze anymore, I close my eyes. Tears pool onto my cheeks, but I don't care anymore. When was the last damn time I let myself cry? If anyone deserves my tears, it's this infuriatingly handsome emo nerd.

"Delete them if you want." My whisper is raspy, like maybe I'm coming down with a cold. "Or you can take a leap of faith that I won't *ever* knowingly hurt you again."

Something solid clatters to Wren's desk, probably

my phone, and then chapped fingers are grazing my cheeks, collecting dampness left from the tears. Soft palms cup the sides of my face, holding me in place, holding me upright, because suddenly my legs are weak. Wren's lips tickle the shell of my ear, and I shiver at their whisper.

"This doesn't mean I forgive you. Not yet, but I'm willing to try." And then their lips are on mine, sealing the deal with the best kiss of my life.

Ben who? is my last thought before losing myself to Wren.

08 A Kiss and a Promise

AN ENTIRE DAY LATER, I swear I can still feel their mouth on mine, those persistent piercings pressing into my bottom lip the entire time we made out. Who knew a manga-reading, Zelda-watching nerd could kiss like that? I hadn't cared about Wren's morning breath or that we were sitting on their bed when Michele found us half an hour later. As soon as she realized I wasn't just a "friend," she'd enforced the open-door policy on us, but we had just laughed it off.

In Wren's house, even with their cranky, bordering on abusive father, we had the best snow day I think I've ever had. I discovered Wren is vegan when everyone got bacon but them, and then after breakfast we played video games. Wren confided in me a little, making me fall inch by inch as they told me of the tense relationship with their brother, Will. When I brought up the scars on Wren's bicep, they visibly bristled, telling me without words that it was a closed topic. I didn't push it, instead hoping one day Wren would trust me enough with their darkest secrets.

Later, gaming turned into cuddling on the floor in Wren's room, and that was when I told Wren about my dad. Their silent acceptance had been everything I didn't know I needed in the moment. When the wind calmed down, I dressed in Michele's snow pants and extra coat and went outside to play in the snow with Wren. I wish I could go back in time and stay there with Wren forever. Or at least until graduation.

I know, I know. Time-travel seems to be a well-played mantra of mine lately.

* * *

As soon as the teacher has her back facing the class during first period, Hayley spins in her seat to face me. "It's been two days, honey. You ever gonna tell us what was up with you at the movies?"

Although I'd been dodging the topic like it was a landmine set to explode, I knew there wasn't a chance in hell I'd escape my nosiest friend. Rehashing the break-up in front of the entire class isn't a goal of mine this morning, and besides, Wren's the one taking up rent in my mind. To say I'm over Ben is an understatement, considering there was nothing to get over in the first place. Except for passing him in the hallway before Housing class, I haven't thought of him once since Saturday. Wren, on the other hand, I couldn't get out of my head if I wanted to. I haven't seen them yet, but that's not uncommon. They usually have an independent study period a couple times a week.

"My god, girl, your eyes just got this sappy, glazed look to them." Hayley smirks, and I blink, unsure how

I'll keep Wren to myself. It's like last week's Tage went on a much-needed vacation, and in her place is a lovesick girl who is … dare I say it? *Happy*.

Gross. I *am* sappy. I make *myself* wanna barf.

"Stop, eyes are on us," I mutter, gesturing with a tip of my head to Ms. Shea frowning down the class at us.

Hayley covers her mouth with her hand, trying to smother her giggle, but continues in an excited whisper. "Did you guys have make-up sex? Did Benny boy keep you warm during the storm?"

"No, and don't be telling people we did, either."

Rolling my eyes, I turn my attention to the front of the class to try to tune her out. No way am I encouraging this to go on. Hayley must be one of the least mature people I know. It's no wonder we ran out of things in common a long time ago.

"Someone's cranky." I hear her pout, her deadpan voice now tinged sour.

I shrug it off, focusing on the assignment Ms. Shea wants completed in two weeks' time. I'm out of my seat as soon as the bell rings, desperate for space from

Hayley and her gossip mill. I'll make it up to her later, but right now there's only one person I want to see.

I spot Wren a few minutes later heading in the direction of the computer room and follow along at a distance. When I finally catch up, I reach to wrap my arms around them before I freeze. For a moment, I forgot where we are. Swallowing, I glance all around to make sure no one is watching before slipping my hand in Wren's. They notice me behind them, and a hesitant smile teases the edge of their mouth. They pull their headphones off.

"Hey, how are you?"

"Come here." Tugging on Wren's hand, I lead them into the darkened computer room. As soon as the door is closed, I'm pulling them into me for a quick kiss. "Better now," I murmur, biting my lip in a smile.

"I've been trying to figure out if this weekend was a prank or not," Wren admits, their forehead resting against mine. "I know you said it wasn't. I–I wanna believe that, because I really like you, Tage."

"I really like you, too." My eyes flutter closed as

I breathe Wren in, the citrus and cedar soap from this morning's shower still clinging to their skin. It's a scent I can't get enough of. "No prank, I promise."

Wren tenses, before pressing a gentle kiss to my forehead. "I believe you believe that, but it's gonna take me some time to believe it too. Just being able to do this," Wren's thumb drags over my bottom lip, and I catch a flash of their crooked grin, "is enough for now."

09 A Day for Hooky

LIFE IS PRACTICALLY PERFECT for the next three days. Romancing Wren is kept on the downlow, mostly to protect them, but also because I'm nowhere near ready to come fully out of the closet. Admitting I'm into Wren was a huge step in the right direction, and Wren must realize how much because they haven't pressed going public. So we send flirty texts through the day, steal kisses behind closed doors, and I spend the rest of my time convincing myself that Wren is more than just a dirty little secret.

It's Friday morning when my near-perfect week takes a slam dunk in the Hillsborough River. Parents, am I right? You can't live with them and … hell, I won't finish that.

"Tage, honey, pull yourself off the island and sit up, for god's sake. Who taught you to eat cereal with your face in the bowl?"

Insert, Mother Dearest. I scowl into my bowl of chocolate Cheerios, ignoring her demand. Shoving another spoonful in, my mouth is chock full as I mumble, "Not you, Constable. Got all my bad habits from the old man."

Her breakfast prep forgotten, Mom comes to stand in front of me, hands on hips. Even pushing forty, she's a looker, with natural blond hair and brown eyes. She keeps fit for her job, but also because she enjoys running and self-defense classes. Why my father left was dirty laundry neither of us cared to air, but my guess is it was because of me and not Mom.

"You got your table manners from him but your attitude from me," Mom corrected, surprising me with a chuckle. She's in a decent mood today, and I'm immediately on edge. We never exchange friendly banter these days.

I go back to my breakfast, and she cracks two eggs into the sizzling pan on the stove. I'm setting my bowl in the dishwasher when she speaks again. "I'm volunteering for the soup kitchen today, in case you forgot. Then I'll be working overnight."

My teeth clench together so hard that my jaw hurts, but I nod, studiously taking in her civilian clothes. How could I forget it's the fourth Friday in the month already? Mom likes to pour her Good Samaritan act on the community twice a month, showering the less fortunate with donations and, more importantly, her time. But when it comes to me? Hells bells, she'll just pull a double shift!

"I know it's a school day, but are you sure you don't want to come help out? It wouldn't hurt for us to do a little bonding." She says it full of hope, like passing out plates of food to strangers is my idea of "good" bonding. My lip curls in a sneer, and I say the same thing I always do.

"No. I live with a stranger already. I don't need to feed more."

***

To make my foul mood worse, my car doesn't start a half hour later. Mom left already, and frankly, I'm still too much in a rage from earlier to care if I miss school. Her blissful ignorance of how fudged-up our relationship is always makes me wonder if she's really that clueless. Is it me? Am I the problem? Is there something about me that has my parents running for the hills? Huffing, I slam my car door and hoof it back to the house. I realize I don't give a damn about that either, not today. I'm in a mood, with an itch to scratch that only sticky fingers can soothe. Before I know what I'm doing, my cell is in my hands and I'm texting Wren.

Tage: Car won't start. Wanna ditch with me today?

Less than twenty seconds later, I get a reply.

Wren: Be over asap, bus just landed at school.

A heavy sigh leaves me, and I instantly feel lighter.

I could have texted an SOS to Aiden, or Hayley, but without thinking I reached out to Wren. There's something about them that calls to me, calming the demons inside. Sounds sappy as hell, but it's actually not so terrible.

I'm slumming it in a pair of my favourite oversized sweats by the time Wren arrives, and I laugh at the slacked look they give me when I open the door. "Never see a girl in sweats, McMillan?"

"I've never seen you in sweats," Wren corrects me, greeting me with a lingering kiss as I kick the door shut.

"What's the verdict?" I murmur, wrapping my arms around their neck. The winter chill lingers on Wren's lips and clothes as I press into them, but I don't mind.

"Tage, I don't think there's a piece of clothing out there that you wouldn't look sexy in."

"Hmm. Good answer."

* * *

We spend the morning curled up on the sofa watching

Netflix before Wren convinces me not only to leave the house but also take transit for the short ride to the Confederation Centre. During the summer, it would be a breeze to walk the ten or so blocks, but since the storm, snow is everywhere.

Wren holds my hand on the bus, and it surprises me how much I don't hate it. We're semiprivate where we're seated, but that usual panic I feel isn't there today. It's nice just to be with Wren. Once we get to our stop, we walk down one more block to Receiver Vic' Row on, you guessed it, Victoria Row. When I was younger, I used to love seeing artsy events put on in the pedestrian street. My parents took me to the library when it was still in the Confederation Centre, and on the way back to the car, we'd always stop to listen to the live music on Victoria Row. Sometimes it was a high school band playing, or jazz, and they would set up on a makeshift stage just before the Richmond entrance into the Confederation Centre. I remember going to quite a few Art in the Open events around town with my dad, loving the one-on-one time while

Mom worked. *That* was bonding, not whatever Mom was attempting.

"I never liked the crowds, so I didn't pay much attention to the festivals," Wren informs me when I ask. "I spent a lot of time at the skatepark with the guys."

We place our order at Receiver before taking a seat right there at the bar counter near the cash. It's wonderfully easy to fall into conversation with Wren, and I find myself telling them about my weekend trips to the library with my dad. Aiden enters the discussion, and Wren comments how she doesn't seem like a complete bitch. Not like Hayley.

It's not long before our bearded attendant is setting our plates in front of us. Wren ordered a peppermint tea and a vegan cookie, and I got a cappuccino, even though I should be cutting carbs with my cheer competition coming up.

Afterward, we head across the pedestrian street to the Confederation Centre's Art Gallery. While we'd both been before, it's awesome to see all the new exhibits set up in the large expanse. Wren looks so at home, like they could blend into the scenery and be forgotten for the weekend. I've never seen them look so happy or in awe as they do studying works of local artists, and it makes me feel weird and mushy. My stomach does an annoying flip when I see them watching me, and my heart races. Gah. What's happening to me?

I'm gah-gah for Wren, that's what, and it's proven when they lead me away from the art gallery an hour later toward our next destination. I'd only just warmed up, so I pout a little, and I quickly learn just how much Wren's deep kisses can act as a heater. I'm still flushed when we hit the first store on Wren's itinerary, a second-hand store called Book Emporium. It's a cute shop with shelves and shelves of well-organized books of all types. Wren manages to find a manga comic they want, and I get a laugh out of the dragon statue mascot near the cash. A note is attached to the dragon's chest, reminding customers not to feed it.

"I'm having a great day with you," I confess, as Wren directs me into Back Alley Music. The places we're going aren't exactly my thing, but it's amazing how little I care what I'm doing when Wren is with me. I wonder if they'd feel the same way watching me cheerlead? I giggle at the thought.

"Me too, Tage. Thanks for texting me and not someone else. I'll look forward to any and all time with you." Wren is riffling through vinyl records, but I can hear the affection in their voice.

I lean against the table, watching Wren for a minute before deciding to open up more. I want their trust, and to get that, I need to give them a piece of me. "I wanted to steal this morning. Had every intention of calling a cab and heading to Walmart. But I texted you instead. It was the best decision I've made in a long time, Wren." I place my hand on their arm, giving it a gentle rub. "I hope you can appreciate what a big deal that is for me."

Wren pulls their attention away from the rock and roll vinyl collection, that crooked, heart-thumping smile all for me, and I gulp, a frightening realization slamming into me. I have absolutely no effing clue what I'm doing. Here I am, begging Wren to forgive me and give me a chance. And here *they* are, handing me their heart and asking me not to break it.

Hells bells, what have I gotten myself into?

10 Keeping Up Appearances

ON TUESDAY, THERE'S A basketball game that I forgot about, and the whole school is allowed to go. Aiden and Jenna are playing, so my friends and I sit at the back of the bleachers to cheer them on. I love special events like this. Anything to get out of class is a win for me. There was a Biology test that I also forgot about, so it'll give me a couple more days to prepare.

Wren is nowhere in sight, but most of the school is in the gym. They don't seem the type to like crowds or sports, so I wouldn't be surprised if they took off early. I never got a text, and even if it's silly or paranoid, I'm always wondering if they're a little pissed at me. It's not every day the person you're dating refuses to acknowledge you. I hate that I'm keeping Wren a secret. The fact is, they mean so much to me already, and I'd be devastated if my friends got wind of our relationship. I'd never hear the end of it from Hayley and Adam, and I'd have to sit back and watch them gleefully chew Wren up and spit them out. So, I hide Wren. Seems petty of me, but it's petty of Hayley for making me feel like I need to in the first place.

"I got money on 26 from the Raiders. She'll score at least eleven points," Ben predicts, leaning over me to hand Hayley a twenty-dollar bill. He grins up at me, and the heavy stubble on his chin reminds me that the boy I grew up with is long gone. The man who replaced him is cocky and determined, and I squirm when his arm grazes my breasts on the way by.

"Why does he need to sit next to me?" I complain, bristling when he does it again. I shove his arm away.

"Quit it, perv."

"'Perv'? Is that any way to treat your first love?"

"Don't flatter yourself, Ben. You're not my first love."

"No?" he murmurs, leaning in close. "Then how do you explain the last two years, almost?"

"A distraction." He could think what he wanted, but as much as I'd sometimes wished it were real, there was never a day where I felt more than friendship with Ben. He was a nice guy most of the time, just with the wrong makeup.

"I figured it'd give you a chance to patch things up," Hayley admits, her face full of playfulness as she tucks another bill into her purse. Every game, the boys make bets on which player will score the most points out of the two teams. "Think about it, if you guys break up, it would seriously ruin the dynamics of our group."

"That's a messed-up way of thinking," I mutter, folding my arms and turning back to the game. I'm not so upset that I'll bother to switch places, but it does hurt that Hayley cares more about how our clique looks than how I feel.

"Aiden's playing strong today," Dylan comments, eyes fixed to the game below. He goes to all Aiden's games, cheering her on louder than anyone in the stands. Sure enough, when she steals the ball from an opponent on the Raiders and takes off down the court, Dylan jumps up to let out an ear-splitting whistle. "Whoop! That's my girl!"

I stifle a laugh, grinning a little. Their cuteness is too much sometimes.

"She is. Aiden's like, the GOAT for the girls' team," I agree, pride evident in my voice. Aiden's a natural athlete, managing to excel at not only cheer but basketball and rugby as well. She's taller than Hayley and me, and more of a tomboy, but it's one of the things I like about her. She doesn't care what people think. Not like I do, anyway, but I guess Aiden doesn't have anything to hide. She's straight, with the most popular guy in school chasing after her.

"Look what the hurricane blew in."

I follow Adam's gaze to the side doors of the gym,

seeing the four students hovering just off the side of the bleachers. But not just any four: Colonel Gray High School's elite band of emo misfits. Half the student body are terrified of them, and the other half think they're attention seekers with mommy issues.

I gnaw my lower lip, getting a good view of Wren when they turn to the bleachers. Watching them with one of their rare grins on display has my breath catching, my heart swooning. I want them to grin at me that way, in front of everyone. They point to an empty place midway up on the bleachers.

"What do they think they're doing? They never come to games." Hayley scowls.

They're here for me, I almost say, feeling my cheeks heat at the thought of Wren going out of their comfort zone to see me. I can't believe they've been all mine for almost two weeks.

"Who cares? Don't let it ruin the game, okay? We're here for Aiden," Dylan says, bending to pull a water bottle out of his bag.

I suck in a breath as Wren spots me sitting at the

top row. I didn't think it was possible, but they look even cuter than they did this morning when I pulled us into the washroom stall before first period. Wren's black toque sits back an inch on their hair, so strands stick out, and the cigarette tucked behind their ear reminds me of their unfortunate nicotine problem. The way they move in those tight, ripped jeans though, has the smoking habit barely on my radar.

I shift my attention to Hayley, wanting to gauge her mood in case I need to intervene or at least offer a distraction, but Adam's doing well to occupy her.

"Hey."

My eyes widen as I notice Wren a couple rows down, trying to get my attention. I hadn't noticed they moved.

"Hey," I return, suddenly feeling like the air is running out inside the gym.

"'Hey'?" Hayley mimics, giving me an odd look before glaring at Wren. "Get lost, freak. You're blocking our view. And you stink."

Hayley insulting Wren is nothing new, but today

I dig my nails in so hard I practically make my palms bleed. I'm torn between wanting to defend Wren and invite them into my circle and keeping them far away from Hayley's toxicity.

Wren's gaze bores into mine, ignoring everyone else. They're so much more confident than me. I can tell years of being bullied has Hayley's words bouncing off Wren's armour. I'm speechless, in complete awe of their silent strength. "Tage, wanna come sit with us?"

Ben and Adam's mocking laughter has me visibly cringing, and, unfortunately, everyone notices. Wren's hazel eyes become shuttered, like the time in class when Hayley ripped up the picture of their mother.

"You must be so obsessed with Tage you've become delusional." Hayley laughs, reaching into her bag of Skittles and throwing one at Wren.

"Yeah, okay."

My throat is on fire as Wren retreats to their seat. I've got a lump lodged there threatening to suffocate me, and my sinuses burn. I haven't felt this worked up since my dad walked out.

As the game moves into the second half, Wren and their friends get up and leave. Watching them go without a backward glance hurts more than I ever thought possible. By not saying anything, I hurt Wren. Again.

When will I learn?

* * *

"So how does a nice girl like you end up running the school with someone like Hayley?" Wren asks after school Wednesday.

Their question baffles me. How can they still think I'm nice after everything I've done? I sip the hot chocolate Wren bought me, giving them a sideways glance, grateful they're still talking to me. "I'm not nice, to be fair. But I get what you're trying to say, and I don't know. Hayley's been my friend so long. One day she just sort of showed up."

"You can be nice. It's in you when you feel like showing that hidden side," Wren gently reminds me. We reach the Lightning Bolt attached to the Confederation Mall, and I smile at their small hand on my lower back as I pull open the door. I don't think they're aware of the contact, but it sends a ripple of goosebumps through me.

"I know I said it already, but I'm so sorry about the other day. You've been uber patient with me so far, and I just … I want you to know I can't wait to show you off. Eventually." We descend the stairs to the basement level where the store is located, and I'm immediately impressed with the mellow vibe at Lightning Bolt. There are only two other people here besides us, and the store design looks like a bunch of geeks got together and had a party.

"I accept your apology," Wren murmurs, acknowledging the guy behind the comic book counter. Wren's hand slips into mine, bringing it to their lips to press a kiss to my knuckles. I swallow hard, mesmerized with how they look at me. Wren brings my hand down but doesn't let go as we browse the comic books. "I saw you and completely forgot what we talked about. I tend to lose my sense when I see you at school," they continue, sipping their own hot chocolate. "I meant what I said. If you need time wrapping your head around this, I'm okay with it. But don't pick on me anymore. I'm over that side of you."

"I promised you I wouldn't."

Wren smiles, for once looking like they genuinely believe me. And when their gaze drops to my lips, I know they want to kiss me. It seems to be their favourite hobby the last couple of weeks, one we can both agree on. "Why do you even like me?"

Wren's hand moves from mine to slip around my waist, tugging me closer to them. With our mouths barely inches apart, they whisper, "Oh, I don't think it's a case anymore of liking you, Tage. What I feel is much deeper than that."

When I stumble inside my house a few hours later, I'm thoroughly kissed and feel more alive than ever. I'm literally buzzing and so full of questions and confessions to my friends, mainly Aiden. I knew for a long time Wren had a crush on me, but I figured if we ever got together, it'd be casual, more for experience than anything. I didn't expect for us to be falling hard for each other so soon.

11 A Secret to Keep

"OKAY, TWO-MINUTE BREAK and then we're back at it. Flyers, get ready!" Leanne hollers at cheer Sunday.

We have a competition coming up in a month, and she's been on edge lately. She'd never say, but I know she doesn't think we're ready. Having an amazing, well-worked routine involves teamwork. Lately we seem to lack in that department.

"Don't drop me this time!" Hayley snaps, glaring at everyone, including me. Especially me, likely. She's been on a rampage all week. Aiden told me Hayley's parents are divorcing, but I can't imagine how that would make her so …

"Bitchy, right? I'm thinking the same thing. She's a legit psycho today."

I turn to see Rain standing beside me with Gatorade in their hand. They look how I feel, like we're about to do cheer stunts with an explosive Angry Bird. I grin, saying, "I'm surprised you're talking to me."

"I have it on good authority you're family now." Rain shrugs, staring ahead, but the corner of their mouth turns up. "And that you're an incredible kisser."

My blush would no doubt make a tomato look pale, and I gawk at Rain. "Wr … Wren said that?"

When I said I wasn't ready to go public, I thought Wren knew it meant everywhere. What if my mom finds out, or my friends? "Oh my god. I feel sick."

"Don't worry, Wren and I are friends. I promised not to tell anyone. You're still so far in the closet Hayley would need a flashlight to find your queerness."

If Rain thought that would make me feel better,

it doesn't. As I get into position with the others to hold Hayley up, I feel disoriented. That millisecond of thinking Wren outed me was all I needed to second-guess our relationship for what must be the hundredth time.

"Tage, are you okay?" Aiden asks as we head to the change rooms after practice.

"You've ditched us all week," Hayley grumbles, still sour I declined her party invite the night before.

"I'm sorry," I say, and I am. I don't want to hurt anyone, but not talking about Wren is next to impossible. I want to dip my toes in the water before jumping in head first. "I've been so busy this week, and my aunt and cousins came to visit."

Another lie, but who's counting anymore?

"I think you've got a secret boyfriend," Aiden teases, stripping off her sweaty t-shirt. Seeing her in just her bra has me whipping around to face the other way. When I finally come out, I don't want my friends to ever feel uncomfortable around me.

"I … I don't, actually." Whew, another truth. Tipping the scale today, go me. Thinking of Wren does weird things to my face though, and a second later I hear Hayley's scoff.

"You don't lie as well as you steal, honey. And whoever is putting that ridiculous cheesy smile on your face, you've gotta let us meet him."

* * *

I'm gonna tell them, I think at lunch the next day.

I swear I will. I'll say, "I'm queer, guys. You'll just have to take me as I am."

And they will.

I mean, they've been my friends for years. We practically grew up together. They must accept me. What kind of friends would they be if they didn't?

"… getting a ride with your mom when we go across? She's coming, right?"

"She's not even listening. Zoned right out."

"Hey! Earth to Tage? Who's living rent free in your head right now?"

I blink, more than once, dusting away the worry

from my mind and failing miserably. I worry all the time. And honestly? I'm not sure what I'm more terrified about — my friends not accepting that I'm queer, or accepting it but not that I'm with Wren.

"Sorry, guys, I must not have gotten enough sleep last night."

Hayley and Aiden give me a long look, something they've been doing a lot of lately. And I get it. I went from mean Tage who was always available to ... well, neither of those things.

Hayley points to my DQ burger, snagging a fry off my tray. "Eat up."

"Okay, Mom."

Aiden takes a sip of her lemonade and runs her fingers through her ginger waves. "We wanted to know the plan for the cheer competition. Are you riding with us? My parents are coming and making me go with them in the van with the brats." The brats being Aiden's twin sisters, Sara and Savannah.

I huff a laugh. "Oh, um, I actually haven't talked to Mom about it yet." I've been so all over the place lately it completely slipped my mind.

Would Wren be into that sort of thing? They know I'm on the cheer team, but besides a brief conversation about hobbies, we never got into it. Wren skateboards and games. Watching a cheer competition would no doubt be a bore for them.

"Well, find out. Maybe I can convince Dad that Hayley and I can ride with you guys."

"Okay."

I spot Wren sitting a few booths down with their friends, Kyle and Jared, and the first thought that comes to mind is, *what would a vegan eat in a place like this?*

I raise an eyebrow when I see an order of onion rings and another of fries in front of them. It's no wonder they're starving after school some days if a tray of empty carbs is the only thing holding them. It doesn't seem like Wren is really paying attention to their friends. They have their head down in their sketchbook and headphones over their ears. I stifle a laugh. They're real social, for sure.

"Jeez, you're gone again," Hayley grumbles, tapping the table with her fingernails. She frowns at me, turning in her seat to see who has my attention. "Please tell me you're at least wasting our lunch looking at the cute baby making a mess with his fries."

"Wren's there," Aiden supplied, a hint of curiosity in her voice.

"God, I'm so over those freaks. I'm headed to the washroom and then we can leave." Hayley grabs her purse on the way out of her seat, stopping to send Wren a look of disgust, but it's a moot point. Wren's lost in their world of illustrations. I bet they don't even know I'm in the restaurant.

"Okay, what's up with you and Wren?" Aiden asks when we're alone. My heart stills at her words, before the pace picks up to a gallop.

This is it.

"Holy! Tage! You're totes simping right now!" Aiden exclaims, her gaze flying back and forth between me and Wren. She slaps my arm and grabs me around the shoulders in a hug, full of barely restrained excitement. "How didn't I see it before? Girl, I am literally shook right now!"

Wren catches us staring and gives me a little grin, holding up their sketchbook. Aiden lets out a squeal. "I'm right, aren't I? Please say I'm right."

"You sound a lot … different than I expected." I expected Aiden to be hesitant and a hundred percent against Wren. The drastic change is oddly nice.

"Say it, say those words, biotch. I'm waiting."

I sigh, looking anywhere but at her. There's no way I'll win this. "I'm dating Wren. And they're amazing," I quickly add as Aiden's jaw drops. I give her a pleading look. "Hayley can't know, okay? Not yet."

"Lips are sealed," Aiden promises, giving my arm a squeeze. Her expression is everything, and I can't help but laugh.

"It feels really good to tell someone."

"You should have told me years ago. My feelings are a tad bit hurt." Aiden pouts, puckering her bottom lip.

"I didn't even know Wren years ago!"

"I mean about you." Aiden does look put out, and for that I'm sorry. I never in a million years thought she'd take me coming out so well. "So … are you like

Rain? You can fall in love with anyone?"

My cheeks flush at hearing the four-letter word tossed into the equation. "I don't think so, at least not with cis boys."

"I was just thinking that. You never looked this happy the whole time you were with Ben." Aiden grins, glancing at Wren as if she's seeing them clearly for the first time. "I don't understand Wren's exact appeal, but I'm happy if you are."

"Thanks, hon. Your love and friendship is so important to me." I give her a quick hug. "I'll be right back. Just gonna say hi really quick."

"Uh-huh. Don't worry about it. I'll make up some excuse for Hayley."

"You're the best." I grab my jacket and purse before making my way across the Dairy Queen. Wren's friends glance up when I land at their table. "Mind if I sit?"

"Mmm, nope." Jared jumps out of his seat, gesturing for me to sit down beside Wren. "Have at it."

"Thanks." When I do, I slide Wren's headphones off

the ear closest to me and lean in. "What'cha drawing?"

Wren cocks their head to me, a crooked grin making their lone dimple pop. "You."

"Oh?" My eyebrows raise, seconds before I get a silly grin on my face. "Really."

"Really, really." Wren opens their sketchbook wider so I can see. Sure enough, a very detailed portrait of me sitting with the girls looks back at me. In the drawing I'm staring off in the distance, my hands folded on the table beside my untouched food.

"Incredible," I say softly, marvelling over every detail. "You even added the mole under my ear."

"Of course. I couldn't leave out the best parts of the portrait."

"Get a room already," Jared mutters, and Wren and I both laugh.

I lace my fingers in Wren's under the table, giving their hand a light squeeze. "Wanna take off?"

12 Lessons to Learn

THEY SHOULD BAN CLASS PRESENTATIONS. The amount of anxiety it brings on a person is neither healthy or necessary. It's not like I'm going to be a teacher or a politician or go into any other career that involves talking in front of a large amount of people. End rant.

Deep breath, Tage.

I stare at the lineup of Bristol board before me, my comic strip glued to the fronts, willing my fingers to stop trembling. Why does it have to be Art class that I share with Wren and Hayley? I'm not even that good. I'd foolishly gone into it in grade eleven thinking I'd make a few sculptures, take a few pictures, and the rest would be a breeze. Hayley pressured me into taking it again this year.

"Go ahead, Tage," my teacher encourages.

I swallow, not daring to look at Wren. If I do, I'll no doubt chicken out. How they even like me, I'll never understand. I lack the emotional and academic maturity to breathe the same air as Wren, let alone be a partner to them. I would have asked for their help, but I was too ashamed to admit I'd left the project until last night.

"C'mon, sexy, do your thang!" Hayley calls out with a whistle.

Grimacing, I silently vow to kill her later. Or at the very least, pay her back for embarrassing me more. "There once was a princess," I begin, moving my hand to the first comic strip, and have to stop to wipe the sweat from my forehead. As I slowly move through the strip, I read off the captions I'd written and typed out to stick on the bottom.

"There once was a princess who everyone envied.

She awed people with her looks, impressed them with her talents, and no one ever complained how she took more than she gave. This princess wasn't nice like in those Disney movies we all grew up watching. She had faults, and emptiness inside her and often wondered if anyone could ever love her for her. She wasn't friends with the forest animals and there weren't magical dishes in her castle, so for much of her life she felt alone."

I pause, wondering if I should go on. My drawing ability is mediocre at best, and it's not clear if the person in the picture is either pretty or a woman. Seriously, it's a step up from a stick-man sketch. Ms. Thompson didn't give us a lot of guidelines when it came to the story aspect, and hearing it out loud, it completely sucks. I feel Wren's eyes on me, drilling holes in me, probably willing me to look at them. When I do, the softness on their face and in those eyes gives me the confidence to continue. My hand hovers over the second Bristol board.

"She had friends, but some couldn't be trusted. They were sly foxes at her back, waiting for her to slip up so they could steal her crown and burn down the castle she'd built. Somehow along the way, she'd accidentally shackled herself to the evil queen masquerading as her friend. And like all evil things, this queen brought out the worst in the princess. One day, a dark knight came along. Not to save the princess as if she were a damsel in distress, but to help her recognize her worth. The knight showed her what it was like to be free, what it was like to feel something besides anger. And even though the knight was feared and misunderstood by many, the princess grew very fond of them. Slowly, over time, she learned to be kind to others, and to herself.

"The end," I finish, hearing the pounding in my ears as the class stares at me. This wasn't like the usual projects I tend to do. Who am I kidding? Most of the time my projects and papers are done by Becky. But Wren has rubbed off on me.

"Well done, Tage," Ms. Thompson says, glancing about the room. She begins a slow clap, and everyone else joins in.

I grab the presentation and slide off my stool, legs wobbly as I make the short distance to my desk. There's a high chance I might still pass out.

"What's with the ending? Is it 'to be continued …'?" Jenna asks, confused.

"Did Becky write that? Because I might need to rethink my business with her." Hayley wrinkles her nose.

I roll my eyes, turning away. My cell vibrates in my sweater, and I hurry to silence it. I forgot I had it on me. I pull it out when Ms. Thompson's not looking, a gush of relief escaping on an overdue sigh.

Wren: I liked the ending the best. Shows promise for the future, like there'll be a part two.

I bite my lip, not daring to look the next row over.

Tage: Me too. Xoxo

Wren: And maybe … I can help with the drawing for the next one?

As soon as I read the text, I burst out laughing.

* * *

"So why didn't we go out for lunch again?" Dylan grumbles, and, like me, he's staring down at the hash on his plate like he's waiting for something to start moving inside the slop.

"You should have got the soup and sandwich, babe." Aiden grins at him, teasing. Holding up half her BLT, she offers him a bite in exchange for a kiss.

"Tage complained about all the fast food we've been eating," Hayley supplies, shoving her plate away and jutting her chin in my direction. Chestnut strands frame her face, exaggerating her already cold blue eyes. "I'm not touching that. It smells like Hank's kibble and looks like throw-up."

Adam chuckles, snaking his arm out to pull Hayley's plate over. Adding it to his portion, he gives it a sniff and shrugs. "I don't mind it."

"Well, you wouldn't. You and your pup have a lot in common."

I snort at Dylan's response, causing milk to slide down my throat the wrong way. I erupt in a coughing/laughing fit in the middle of the cafeteria, watching through misty eyes at the smirks on my friends' and frenemies' faces.

"It wasn't that funny. Quit being so *extra*," Jenna mutters at the other end of the table.

"Caught me off guard," I wheeze, reaching for the napkin to wipe moisture from my eyes. In the process, I get an eyeful of Jenna boldly rubbing her fingers along my ex's arm. Aiden told me that Ben and Jenna had been hanging out non-stop since the basketball game, so he clearly couldn't have been that into me. With Jenna occupying him now, at least he won't be trying to get back together, so it's all good. As a bonus, Jenna might forget she's got a strange obsession with Wren.

"Anyone else notice Tage has a semi-permanent smile stuck to her face lately?"

I sip my milk, trying to smooth down the scratchiness in my throat before taking a cautious bite of my food. Thankfully, it doesn't taste as awful as it looks, and I shrug Hayley's comment off. "What about you? It's lunch time, and you haven't made anyone cry yet. Your ego booster come as a juice shot today?"

Okay, what was that?

Aiden lets out a low whistle, giving her head a slight shake toward me, a clear warning in her blue eyes. "Leanne scheduled an extra practice for tomorrow. Did you see that email?"

"How can you tell Tage is smiling? She has her resting bitch face on," Adam remarks, squinting at me from across the table. After several seconds of making me squirm, he gives up with another shrug. "Looks the same to me."

"So you're looking for someone to cry, are you?" Hayley drawls, propping her elbow on the table and her chin in her hand. She bats her long lashes at me. "I knew we were friends for a reason. You're like the PB to my jelly."

I cock my head, briefly confused by how she managed to take what I said as a compliment. I spot the class geek coming toward our table, likely giving me the assignment I paid her to write for me for English class. Weeks ago, before Wren and I became ... well, whatever we are. My stomach tightens as I realize the predicament I'm in. If Becky hands me the assignment, I'm no better than I've always been. If I don't accept it, I risk flunking the semester.

My eyes widen as Hayley sticks out her foot, tripping Becky in the middle of the cafeteria. Books and duotangs fly from her arms as she stumbles, eventually falling into Jenna's lap.

"Eww, get off, you cow!" Jenna shoves Becky away and I watch in horror as the girl falls to the floor.

And then Wren is there, blocking Becky from Jenna's view and glaring at my friends. I swallow, very aware of my heart thudding inside my chest as their gaze collides with mine. Wren is glaring at *me*.

"Leave her alone."

Wren's normally honeyed voice is hard, unflinching, and a secret part of me is proud of them for taking a stand. I didn't ask for *this*, for Hayley to bully someone today. I had just been making an observation ...

Becky's freckled cheeks are flushed as she stares up at me from the floor, deep wells of tears already running. Emotion is thick on my tongue, so thick the shame for Hayley's actions makes it impossible to speak. I glance away, unable to handle both Becky and Wren's disapproving looks.

"Becky, is everything okay here?" a teacher asks.

My head hangs low, the prick of tears in my eyes threatening to spill at another's expense. Maybe I *am* different now. Being close to Wren the last couple of weeks has made me feel different, better somehow.

"Becky's fine, aren't you, honey?" Hayley coos, her teacher's pet façade oozing with sweetness. Sticking her hand out, she offers to help Becky up.

"I … I'm fine. Clumsy, I guess," Becky mumbles, letting Hayley and the teacher help her to her feet, but it's Wren I'm peering at. They've gone ahead and started picking up all of Becky's books that she dropped, and then another student bends to help as well. Completely numb, I slowly slide off my seat to help out, too.

"You've done enough," Wren hisses, purposely picking up the textbook I was about to grab.

"Wren …" A duotang with my name on the front catches my attention, and my voice trails off. I reach for it but the random kid helping us scoops it up between two others. I clench my jaw, a steely determination coming over me. I refuse to flunk out. I'm *getting* that assignment, one way or another.

13 Actions Have Consequences

I DECIDE TO SKIP ENGLISH CLASS, not nearly prepared for the Shakespeare crap and absolutely avoiding Wren, who's also in the class. After the incident with Becky, I couldn't focus at all in Biology and epically failed a pop quiz. Wren's pissed-off face is a screen saver in my mind, showing up each time I blink or if I daze for too long. The nervous butterfly stomach jitters are gone, and in their place a feeling that's so much worse. The sickness pulsing through me makes everything hurt, from my stomach to my head to my heart. I feel it the deepest there. I need to go home, maybe take a bath, cry a little. Because that's what I do. I torment people and then cry like a baby.

I slow to a stop when I see Becky at her locker between classes. She must be running late because the hallways are pretty much deserted by now. I've got my coat on and bag around my shoulders, but I watch her down the hall. She isn't paying attention to me, which is good because I can't come up with a good enough thing to say to her. Somehow, 'sorry' doesn't come close. And yet, the evil part of me is just begging to reappear, only caring about the missing assignment.

My eyes narrow, all that energy I'd lacked moments before rushing to the surface. I watch her dial the lock combination back and forth, but I memorized it ages ago. I zone in on the cash leaving her jeans pocket and disappearing in her locker, along with her Chemistry book and those three duotangs. As soon as she leaves, and the hallway is clear, evil Tage takes over. I'm at Becky's locker, punching in her code — 6-23-10, easy-peasy. The cash is lifted in seconds.

Mine.

I spot the duotang meant for me nestled between Becky's Chemistry and English books, and I quickly lift that off her as well, a silly grin on my face. My adrenalin is soaring now, satisfied I've indulged and proud I've taken back what's mine. I close the locker. I'm turning away when I spot Wren at the other end of the hallway, near my locker, a deep frown on their face.

Scenarios of Wren coming to apologize, or even just to pretend lunch didn't happen and go straight to kissing me race through my head, and I hurry to close the distance between us. They're wearing a jacket, too, like maybe I wasn't the only one about to skip class.

"Wren, hey. I can explain."

"Explain, really? I'd love to hear it." Wren folds their arms in front of them, probably so I can't get as close. That stubborn jaw is set, hazel eyes darker now that they're angry again. "Explain why you need to break into someone's locker and steal."

I clear my throat, swallowing the burn there

again. I can't look at Wren as I mutter, "Becky had my homework, I ... I ... I paid for it. I need it."

Wren's hand palms my cheek, sliding down to tilt my chin up so I have nowhere else to look but at them. Confusion and regret on Wren's face has me choking up, that same remorse I felt in the cafeteria slamming into me full force.

"Wren ..." I rasp, blinking back alien tears. I *never* cry in front of people, but today I can't stop.

"Becky MacDonald? You're breaking into her locker after watching her get shoved to the floor? She cried all last period because of what you and your friends did, Tage. Maybe ... maybe I don't know you at all."

* * *

I never imagined I could feel so miserable.

I'd spent so long taking my problems out on others to make myself feel better that at some point I must have turned a blind eye to the extreme lengths

Hayley's been taking. Or has it just never bothered me this much? Certainly not enough to stop the bullying.

Maybe it's Wren's disapproval eating away at me, not my own guilt at the things I've done.

"Can't sleep, honey?"

I flinch, swinging my gaze up from my tea to find Mom standing in the kitchen's entrance. She's in her pajamas, watching me as she fastens the belt to her housecoat. It's cold in the house tonight, but that's how Mom likes it. She says it's a waste of money cranking the heat before bed.

It's been ages since we've said more than a few passing words to each other, and I falter, unsure of what to tell her. "Kettle's still hot, if you want some tea."

Mom's smile is soft, her eyes full of tenderness I didn't know she was still capable of. "Tea sounds lovely. Are there any of those cookies left I bought the other day at Buns and Things?"

I tilt my head toward the pantry. "I think I only had one."

"So what's got you awake at three in the morning?"

I sip my hibiscus tea, waiting for Mom to take a seat beside me at the island. She grabs a cookie, taking a bite before sliding the tray over. Sticking my hand in, I move two cookies aside to pick one with more chocolate chips. "Just … you know, school drama."

"Okay," she says slowly, biting into her snack. Crumbs fall onto the island, a sign of how old the cookies are. "Can we narrow it down a bit? Are you having Ben trouble? Classes going okay?"

"No, it's not like that." Technically, those play a hand in my issues, but … "Do you think I'm a good person?" I freeze, hyperaware of how wide my eyes must be despite exhaustion making it hard to hold my head up. I force out a laugh, shrugging off my insecurity. "Never mind, I know the answer. Please don't answer that."

"What has you doubting that? Of course you're a good person, Tage."

"No, I'm *not*, Mom!" My chest feels too tight as I scrape the stool away from the island and climb off. Emotion swells, more than I've felt for a long time, and I continue in a strangled voice. "I'm actually a pretty terrible person, but you'd know that if you were ever home."

"Um … okay. I'm sorry you feel that way, honey. But you know … I'm here now, willing to listen."

I shake my head as a tear slips out, and it splashes onto my cheek. It makes me think of fighting with Wren all over again, and I sob. I finally let them in a little, and it's over before it really began. "Forget it, okay? I'm going to bed."

"Tage, please. Let me —"

I swivel around to face her, breathing hard. The urge to hurt her is strong, like she's been hurting *me* since Dad left. Pieces of the truth bubble out like a soda that's been shook too many times, my voice blaring enough to wake the neighbours.

"I'm freaking queer, Mom! Like rainbows, parades, Ellen-level *queer* as can be, and I'm so damn *tired* of spending all my energy trying to hide it!"

I'm glaring, daring her to pull a Dad move and change the subject. Anxiety has my gut twisting, but there's also a strange sense of relief now that I've told her. Like a huge weight's lifting off my too-tense shoulders.

My eyes narrow to slits as Mom moves off the chair, following her every move as she makes her way cautiously over to me. Not an ounce of anger or judgment radiates from her. If anything, her expression now has an almost nauseating tenderness to it. She wraps her arms around my rigid posture, planting a light kiss on my cheek as more tears fall.

"I can tell you've been holding that in for a very long time. I … I can't even begin to tell you how sorry I am and I'm ashamed you felt you had to hide. I would have told you to ditch Ben long ago."

I laugh between sobs, my body going slack against her strong frame. I bury my face into the crook of her neck, letting the wasted years of fear, pain, and rejection from my father unload onto my mother in a messy blend of tears and snot.

"Mom?"

"Right here, honey. Always," she murmurs, kissing my head and holding me tighter.

I squeeze her back, tilting my face to meet hers. Her eyes are full of warmth, full of love for me. How had I missed it for so long? "I think I want to volunteer with you next time. At the soup kitchen. You know, to bond."

Mom throws her head back and laughs, and I know we're in the beginnings of something great again.

14 Friends and Foes

"OOOH, HAVE YOU SEEN this one yet?" Aiden taps my shoulder, and I haven't even turned my head yet before she's shoving her phone in my face.

I stare at the screen, watching as a cat dances to whatever old-school music is playing. It sounds like something my mom listens to. "Cool."

"Funny, right? Cats are so smart! You should train Bruno to do stunts like this." Aiden flops down on the bed with me, where I've been sulking for the better part of an hour. Bruno is curled into me, purring. When Aiden gives him a little scratch under the chin, he leans into her hand, demanding more. She giggles, giving in and stroking his black fur. My precious boy has never lacked affection in three years, but he likes to put on a show for guests so they feel bad for him. "You're a good boy, aren't you, baby? And so handsome!"

"Careful, he might wanna go home with you. And then who would I have to snuggle with?" I mutter, my voice husky from pent-up emotion. Tears blur my vision, but I refuse to let them fall.

Aiden leans her head on my shoulder, causing my body to involuntarily shudder. Her unwavering friendship has the deep ache inside me threatening to crack open. "Wren still hasn't texted back?"

I give a slight shake of my head. My throat is raw, and I need to swallow a few times before I can whisper, "I think … I think it's done. They're done."

"After one fight?"

Reaching for Bruno, my fingers tremble as I stroke his silky soft fur. "After what I did. I … was an idiot."

Aiden scoffs. "I can't see how they'd give up on you that quick. Wren's been into you for a long time, Tage. Long enough to notice all your quirks and illegal activities."

"Doesn't make —" I take a deep breath, trying again. "Doesn't make ... what I've done right."

"So apologize to Becky at school tomorrow. And to Wren, face to face. You know I never liked you stealing, Tage. I just figured it was to rebel against your mom because she's a cop and eventually you'd stop."

I cut my eyes from her compassionate gaze. Aiden really is a good friend, so unlike Hayley. It shames me it's taken so long to realize it. "I won't do it anymore."

Aiden rubs my back. "That's the best news I've heard all day."

"It's long overdue."

"Mmm. And Tage? We need to talk about Hayley. Because she's out of control."

* * *

I usually meet the girls in the parking lot each morning and we go into school together, but I don't feel like putting on a fake face so soon after this weekend, so I head inside alone. My mom holding and consoling me, after a solid year or two of barely speaking and touching, was a steep hollow I didn't know I needed filling. And the way Aiden came through for me was a level in our friendship I never thought possible. I can trust her with my secrets, my heart, and believe she won't talk about me behind my back.

Although my relationship with Wren is currently in shambles, I'm lighter inside somehow. Whatever happened has me feeling like I got some sort of upgrade.

Walking through the halls toward my locker this morning is an eye opener for me. I've been a student here almost three years and it's as if I'm noticing things for the first time. People aren't creating a path for me because they look up to the popular girl. The truth has me abruptly stopping, scanning the handful of faces around me. When I land on a tenth grade boy I recognize, I give him a small wave. "Hey, weird question. Are you afraid of me?"

He says nothing, but sometimes silence is a dead giveaway. What kind of person am I that kids fall back when they see me coming? I'm not a good person, *yet*. But I can change. Nothing seems as important today as it was a few days ago.

My mom *knows*.

Somehow, her acceptance was evil Tage's undoing. I don't want to be her anymore. I wanna be a girl Wren wants to get to know. Hell, I want to be someone *I* wanna get to know. Self-love and all that, right?

"Eli, someone's getting their ass kicked in the student parking lot!"

I blink, focusing on the younger guy who joins me and 'Eli' in the hallway. I clear my throat, giving away my presence. "Anyone noteworthy?"

A few fights break out every year, but it's not my thing. I never get off on physically hurting anyone. Emotional damage is where my talent lies.

Correction. *Was*. Past tense.

"Whoa, you're a babe," the kid gushes, and I stifle a laugh as his face turns multiple shades of red when he realizes he's spoken out loud.

"Thank you. You're very sweet," I reply, raising an eyebrow as he continues to gawk at me. Finally, I snap my fingers and repeat, "Who's fighting?"

"Oh, uh … that emo girl."

The bottom of my stomach drops out as Wren's face comes to mind. There are only a handful of emo students, and all except one are boys.

I don't bother explaining to the kid that Wren identifies as nonbinary. I just take off down the hall to the nearest exit. By the time I reach the parking lot I've done the equivalent of a warm-up and it takes a little bit to catch my breath. A group of spectators are heading toward the parking lot, and I race past on my way to Wren. I finally reach the crowd and shove my way inside to the centre, instantly spotting Jenna and another girl on top of Wren on the ground.

"Hey, honey, come to watch the show?" Hayley grins at me from her place inside Adam's Jeep. The window is open despite the snowflakes getting in, and the engine is running. I spin around, scanning all the faces but not seeing Aiden or Dylan anywhere.

Did she know about this?

Impossible. She would have told me, that's one thing I'm sure of.

"What are you *doing*? Jenna, get off Wren!" I shout, heart thrashing in my chest. For the first time in my life, the possibility of *not* helping Wren isn't even on my radar, just the soul-crushing desire to protect them. I rush in to break up the fight, horrified to see Wren curled up in a ball on the ground as the girls hit them. Wren is past losing, their arms wrapped around their head to ward off the blows.

I manage to pull one girl off, and when I get between Jenna and Wren her fist barrels into my face. I suck my teeth, ignoring the sting, and glare up at Jenna. Shoving her back, I snarl, "Wren is off limits! This fight is *over!*"

My friends are witnessing this new side of me, and I'm not sure they like it. Still, they all stand down, and for what feels like forever, I hover over Wren and watch the crowd disappear. Without a fight to watch, they have nothing better to do now than go to class. Hayley and Adam leave as well, sending me curious, predatory glances as they drive away.

"Tage, you're here."

Wren's low, pain-filled voice is full of disbelief. When I pull their arms down to see pride in their eyes, I know I did the right thing.

"Let me get a look at you," I choke, my gaze roaming over every inch of them and ashamed to find new tears pricking my eyelids. With Wren's bomber jacket on and no noticeable tears in the clothes or broken bones, it's tricky to figure out if the splatter of blood on the ground is coming from anywhere but their face. Pulling gloves from my jacket, my hands shake as I use one to wipe blood from Wren's lip, cheek, and nostril. The sight of the torn-out hoop piercing makes my stomach lurch. "I'm so sorry, Wren."

"Hey, don't cry." Wren struggles to a sitting position, pulling me into them. I selfishly sink into their lap, needing the closeness Wren offers. Leaning my head against their shoulder, I snuggle into their neck and am instantly comforted by the feel of their pulse under my touch.

Wren reaches a hand up to stroke my hair, my cheek that's already swelling from Jenna's massive fist. "I can't believe you did that for me. Hayley's gonna —"

"I don't care," I cut in, raising my eyes to greet the worry on Wren's face. The concern for me is sweet, but hurting Wren feels worse than anything Hayley could do to me.

There's no mistaking the agonized groan against my lips as Wren bends to kiss me, but when I go to pull away the arms around me tighten slightly. "Not yet," Wren murmurs, sliding their hand from my hair to cup my chin, holding me in place. Bursts of heat waves and tingles awaken me, and by the intense way Wren's watching me, I know they feel it, too.

"You need a doctor," I gush, darting my tongue out to wet my chapped lips. My heart is racing, for a whole different reason this time, and I reluctantly tug out of Wren's grasp. When I help them up, I watch the way Wren favours one leg. "I'm gonna make sure Jenna gets expelled for this."

My eyes narrow as Wren just smiles through the pain.

"What?"

Shrugging, they tighten the arm around me in a sideways hug. "I don't care," Wren admits, repeating what I said earlier. Chuckling, it ends in a loud groan as they choke out, "I got the girl. I've already won."

15 Breaking Free

THE HOSPITAL NOTIFIES Wren's parents despite them pleading against it, and I can guess why as soon as Mr. McMillan charges into the ER.

"Another fight, Wren? Who was it this time?" he booms, spittle flying from his mouth as he makes angry gestures with his hands, completely uncaring of the packed waiting room. He's a big man, tall and heavyset, and full of hard edges. A little scary on a good day, but now? I wish I had called my mom in as backup.

"Look at me when I'm talking to you, girl." Mr. McMillan pries Wren's hand away from holding a tissue to their nose.

"You don't have to be here. I'm sure Michele would've come," Wren mutters. Without the tissue to soak it up, blood drips onto their jacket again. The nosebleed hasn't stopped the whole time we've been here, the torn piercing hole or the nostril in general. I'm worried it's broken.

Without thinking, I lean into Wren and tug their hand free. "The fight wasn't Wren's fault."

Whew, my heart's racing! I don't know what's gotten into me, but I could get used to this new habit of defending people.

"Sir, if you can't calm down, I suggest you walk it off," a guard warns, beside us now. He has one hand on his radio, and another on his belt buckle.

"Oh, I'll go. I can't even look at you right now," Mr. McMillan sneers, nudging Wren's Converse with his foot. He scoffs at the many doodles and tributes to My Chemical Romance etched into Wren's sneakers.

"When you get home, your ridiculous goth phase is over. Is that understood?"

"Emo."

"What was that?"

Wren stares up at their father, the bruises and swelling around their eyes catching the fluorescent lighting. The agony in Wren's hazel eyes has me reaching for their hand, not missing the way Mr. McMillan glares at me. He must be queerphobic, too.

"Emo, not goth. And emo is Wren's lifestyle, not a phase," I announce, tilting my chin up so he can get a good look at my resting bitch face. I'm finally putting sassy Tage to good use.

It looks like he wants to argue further, but when the security guard clears his throat loudly, Mr. McMillan shakes his head and storms outside again.

I let out a breath, turning to Wren. "Your dad is terrifying."

"He doesn't like who I've become." Wren grimaces, avoiding my gaze. A lot of patients are still watching us, and the audience has Wren lowering their voice even more. With the tissue back on their nose, it comes out sounding nasally. "I lost count ... how many times he asked if I had a boyfriend over the years. Being queer *and* emo ... he's ashamed."

"Well, he's missing out on knowing you. Just like I was for the longest time," I murmur, pressing a kiss to Wren's shoulder and wishing we were alone. I rest my head where my lips just were and cross one leg over the other. There is quite a bit of attention on us, but none of it seems to be negative. An older couple is even smiling at us across the aisle, and their acceptance gives me hope. I could get used to this — being with Wren in public, and holding them.

Wren's lips graze my forehead. "I love you, Tage."

* * *

Stealing has always been a bit of a crutch for me when I'm upset, so not being able to do that has me driving around aimlessly hours later. Michele showed up at the hospital just as Wren was going into a back room, so I stayed in the waiting room until they were seen by the doctor. Now that Wren's at home resting, with ice on their bruised ribs, I find myself in the student parking lot at school.

What am I doing here?

I don't remember the drive, and for a minute I just sit inside the Camry, keys in hand, staring at the smear of Wren's blood on my door handle. One of my best friends planned for Wren to get hurt, and I need to know why. It shouldn't matter, but it does. How could Hayley hate someone so much she'd plan an attack on them? Wren said they were cutting through the parking lot when they were jumped.

The new notification Wren set up on my phone of their favourite song by The Used goes off, the fluctuating rhythm of the chorus filling my purse. I pull it out, an instant smile on my face as I read the text.

Wren: You didn't say it back, but it's OK. Today you showed me.

Tage: It's 2 soon for you to know.

I put my phone away, not waiting for Wren's reply,

but the smile on my face is anything but low key. Is it possible to love someone you've only been with a short time? Because being with Wren is making me do all kinds of things I never thought possible.

I pocket my keys and head into the school. It's nearing the end of second last period, and soon Hayley and Aiden will be going to Gym.

My reasons for coming back in the first place become clear. As the bell rings and students pile out of classrooms, I don't stroll through the halls of my school. I *stalk* them, hunting for my target in each of Hayley's hangouts.

I find the group of them in the gym change rooms, Aiden noticeably quiet and standing apart from the rest of Hayley's friends. The clanging of the door against the brick wall has all the girls turning toward me.

"Tage!" Aiden exclaims, rushing to me as she tugs on her t-shirt. Her eyes are full of questions. "How's Wren? I had no idea that would happen."

I open my mouth to reply, but Hayley and Jenna interrupt us. "Since when do you stand up for that makeup-smeared freak?"

"How's your face?" Jenna asks with a chuckle. "I didn't know you'd jump in front of Wren, sorry."

I touch my cheek at the reminder, frowning at the medical wrap fastened around Jenna's wrist. The anger I came in here with fades, leaving me with a deep sadness — for myself, for taking so long to realize Wren was never the problem, and for them. They still don't see how toxic they are.

"I came in here for …" My voice trails off as my gaze collides with Hayley's. I give her a helpless shrug. "I don't even know, to be honest. But I'm done with you, Hayley. I've hidden behind your shadow for so long that it took years for me to remember I have one of my own. I'm taking it back."

I reach for Aiden, squeezing her hand before opening the door once more. I glance back at the stunned looks on Hayley and Jenna's faces. "Oh, and Wren and I are a couple. So back off."

16 Secret No More

SITTING KNEE TO KNEE with Wren at the table while we study has to be the most torturous thing I've ever done. I've always struggled holding my attention on tasks, but now I'm thinking the lack of focus might have been selective.

"What's your favourite thing to do in the summer?"

Wren lifts their eyes to mine, pen hand poised over the scribbler they're taking notes in. For a moment Wren watches as I trace my fingers over their forearm.

"Skateboard, eat ice cream, chill down at Peakes, and people watch. I like to draw the tourists coming off the cruise ships."

I smile, enjoying that mental image all too much. Wren must have stacks of binders filled with drawings hidden in their closet. "You should set up a stand and charge for each drawing."

"I'm too shy for that," Wren sheepishly confesses, like it's a trait I didn't already know about.

"I guess." Wren's other hand lands on mine, their fingers ghosting over mine on their arm. It might have taken some time for Wren to trust I won't hurt them, but it was hours of talking and listening I wouldn't trade for anything. The connection we have, I think it's always been there. Ever since I first saw them in my school last year. They were new, totally out of place, and the only openly noticeable queer. There were a few other students out in grade twelve at the time, but thankfully none that caught Hayley's attention.

Wren's t-shirt sleeve has ridden up, and I zero in on the faint scars marring the pale skin of their biceps. As much as we've done together in the last several weeks, I've yet to see Wren shirtless. My burning curiosity must be showing on my face, because Wren picks up my hand and presses a sweet kiss over my knuckles. "Fourteen was a hard year for me," they quietly explain.

Our gazes collide, and I'm taken aback by the regret in Wren's. Their eyebrows are creased together, deep in thought, and their long lashes slowly blink. I panic at the vulnerability in Wren's hazel eyes, watching the way their irises shift greener than their usual tinges of golden brown. "You don't need to tell me, it's okay."

Wren gives me a small, grateful smile, reaching up to tuck a strand of hair behind my ear. "There's not much to tell," they murmur. "I was depressed and lashing out in every way. Started cutting myself as a coping mechanism but found out it was hard to stop. Ended up in the hospital for a couple weeks, and therapy, and then Michele came along." Wren's smile widens at the mention of their stepmom, a hint of a twinkle back in their eyes.

"Michele's a great person," I agree, grateful to

finally know what happened. I'm sure Wren's recap is a condensed version, but it doesn't matter. The important thing is that Wren overcame the darkness so many of us face and is here today. I lean in for a kiss, whispering, "Thank you for telling me. Now, tell me, what's your favourite flavour?"

Wren chuckles at the random topic change, but I don't want them stuck in the past if I can help it. "What? Of ice cream?" They're teasing, undeterred by my endless questions. I can't help it. I want to know them from the inside out. On one date I'm sure I asked Wren thirty questions in the span of an evening, but they never got annoyed. "That's easy. Ben & Jerry's dairy-free Mint Chocolate Cookie. It's the closest I've found to the Chunky Chocolate Mint I used to eat at Cows. What about you?"

"Well," I say slowly, silently running through the list of flavours offered at our island's most famous ice-cream shop. "First of all, I only like the ADL and Cows brand."

"That's fair."

I bite my lip. Decision making is always an ordeal for me. Mom used to joke it's because I'm a Libra. "I'd say ... either Gooey Mooey or the Moo York Cheesecake."

"Mmm, the Moo York Cheesecake is delish." Wren nods appreciatively. They lean in to press a kiss against the corner of my mouth before reminding in a teasing whisper, "We have a test tomorrow."

"Okay, okay."

We spend another half hour running through what happened in *Macbeth*. Wren is a much better student than I am, and I love listening to their perception on the Shakespeare play. It almost makes the gibberish worth it.

"Have you heard anything yet from UPEI?"

I close my books and give a long stretch. "No, but even if I did get in, I'd probably need a tutor. I doubt there'd be a Becky so readily available, and besides," I add with a shrug, "I'm done with that."

"I'm happy to hear it." Wren grins, and the slight dimple in their cheek is a sexy focal point to their smile.

How am I falling for you so fast?

It's true. Spending time with Wren is the highlight of each day, and I care for them … possibly more than I have anyone. It's a terrifying feeling, one I just wish I had the guts to scream from the rooftops. Wren hasn't told me they love me again, but I don't mind. I get the feeling that, as usual, they're waiting for me to catch up.

"Your nose is looking better," I murmur, studying Wren's face again. After a week the cuts have already closed over and turned to scabs, the bruises fading. The same goes for Wren's ribs, thankfully. Wren isn't a large person — in fact, I'd wager I'm heavier and stronger than them — and the way they'd been hardly able to catch their breath after the fight had me worried something was broken.

The front door opens and closes, and a moment later I can hear my mom stripping out of her jacket and boots. "Someone order a delivery?"

Mortified by how loud she is, I duck my head away from the laughter in Wren's eyes. "God, are you sure you want to meet her?"

"Too late now."

"Hey guys!" Mom greets us as she bombards her way into the kitchen.

"Hi."

We watch as my mom drops the bags of takeout onto the island before padding in sock feet over to us at the table. She juts her hand out for Wren to take, and I'm grateful I thought to give her a heads-up of my guest. "Wren McMillan. So glad to meet you. Is your father Russel, by chance?"

"Really, Mom?"

Mom either thinks she knows everyone or *needs* to know everyone. She's usually right. In her line of work, I imagine it would help.

"You didn't do a criminal record check again, did you?"

Wren just laughs, shaking Mom's hand. "That's him."

* * *

The next morning, I wake to my phone chiming and vibrating off my nightstand as numerous messages come in. A long, sleepy groan escapes from somewhere inside me and I nuzzle back into my pillow, pulling the covers over my head to get a few minutes more shut-eye. Wren and I had FaceTimed for hours last night, talking and catching up on episodes of *Bridgerton*. Considering Wren loves loud music and darker, more punkish things, them being obsessed with the show was an awesome surprise.

"Why are you always on my mind?" I mutter from under the covers, rolling my eyes as my lips curve into a smile. My body is a constant bundle of nerves, uncontrollable happiness and weak-kneed anticipation these days, thanks to Wren McMillan.

My cell goes off again, and this time I stick my arm out of my warm cocoon to check the screen. My eyes widen as I notice the time. "Shoot, I'm late!"

Throwing the blankets off, I almost send Bruno soaring across my bedroom. He lets out an annoyed meow at the intrusion. It's a good thing he has mad reflexes and lands on all fours. "Sorry, boy!"

I jump in the shower quickly, not wasting more time than I have to blow-dry my hair. I do however, slow down to my usual morning pace to put on a little makeup. Nothing over the top, just eyeliner and cherry lip gloss. Puckering my lips in front of the mirror, I smile, noting how lively my blue gaze is compared to a couple months ago. I'm *happy*, like, deliriously so.

Being with Wren and living life for *me* for once has been a game changer in regards to my self-esteem. I hadn't realized just how damn depressed I'd been the last few years.

I assess the outfit I chose, ripped blue denims and one of Wren's casual yet comfortable MCR hoodies. Although it's baggy on them, it fits me perfectly. It'll be Wren's first day back to school since the fight, and my first day 'out and proud,' so I figured if I wore something of theirs it'd give me a bit of confidence. Besides, the hoodie smells like them.

Super cheesy, I know.

I rush to finish getting ready, checking messages as I make my way downstairs to the kitchen.

Aiden: We'll meet you there. Xxo

Tage: Thanx so much!

Mom's already rushing around with a slice of toast between her teeth as she pours soup into a Thermos. She's in uniform, her gun holstered to her waist.

She looks up when she sees me. "Morning, honey! You slept in, too?"

"Uh-huh. Morning." I yawn, heading for the coffee pot and pouring some into my Thermos. I set it on the island long enough to pull on my coat and boots. "Sorry, Mom, but I've gotta go."

"Yeah, me too. Here." She hands me a banana and granola bar, bending to kiss my forehead. She smiles. "Love you, honey. Drive safe."

"You too."

Wren is waiting patiently for me when I pull into their drive, seeming out of place while makeup-free. Mr. McMillan was true to his word when Wren returned from the hospital, making them get rid of all their emo-related things. It's a good thing he didn't check the garbage bins for proof afterward.

As soon as Wren's in the car they reach across the console for me, wrapping an arm around my shoulders, and bringing their mouth to mine for a kiss. "Morning, beautiful."

"Hi." I smile, kissing them back. I reach for the toiletry bag in my backseat, dropping it in Wren's lap before reversing out of the lane. "All your makeup is in there. I'll drive easy so you can put it on."

"Tage, seriously, babe, you're the best." Wren's relieved grin has me on top of the world already, and the day is just beginning.

When we reach school, my stomach is twisting like the last time I drank too much at Hayley's party. Doubt and fear have me digging in my heels at the front doors, and if not for Wren's comforting hand reaching for mine, I think I'd be running halfway back to Brighton Road by now. Right on schedule, Aiden and Dylan push through the doors as well and stand beside us. Turns out, I wasn't the only one who outgrew Hayley and the rest.

"Who's ready to turn some heads?" Dylan jokes, slinging an arm around my shoulders.

"You can do this," Aiden adds, squeezing my hand

for extra reassurance.

I take a long, deep breath before slowly exhaling. I turn to Wren. "Remember what you said to me at the hospital?"

Wren's knowing gaze implodes into mine. "Yep. Still mean it, too."

I reach for their hand, and together, the four of us start down the hall. "Well … so do I."

"I know. You can do this, Tage."

I nod. Yes, I can.

Finally, for the first time in my life, I'm brave enough to leave behind the toxic parts and embrace all the good things in my life. I'm letting evil Tage go, once and for all. I'm a good person, and it's about time I let others see through me. Just as Wren has all along.

For the first time in my life, I'm right where I'm supposed to be.

I'm *who* I'm supposed to be.

ACKNOWLEDGEMENTS

I'd first like to thank my wife for always supporting me, no matter which direction I take in life. I love you and thank you for believing in me and my writing.

A huge thanks goes out to James and the rest of the gang at Lorimer for giving me this opportunity. I've enjoyed working on the Real Love series and am excited to see what else the future has in store.

To my beta readers, Paige and Ava. Thank you for loving Tage and Wren as much as I do and for giving honest feedback through a YA POV. Love you girls!

A special thanks to Allister, the best editor I could ever have been introduced to. *Secret Me* wouldn't be here if it weren't for you. You're kind and always have words of encouragement coming my way whenever I'm doubtful of the story. I hope we get to work on many more projects together!

To my kids, especially Colten. Thanks for hearing me ramble on about all my characters and only occasionally getting confused over which book I'm talking about!

And to YOU, the reader. Thank you. Thank you for picking up this book, for taking a chance on me as an author. *Secret Me* is my first YA book, but high-school bullying is as old as time itself. Please, embrace Tage's story and the lessons she learns. High school is hard on most people, but living your truth could be the best thing you ever did for yourself.

Much love,
Angel